OTHER BOOKS BY SHEILA WRIGHT

BON COURAGE, MES AMIS!
Thoughts on restoring a rural ruin

Published May 2002
Reprinted June 2003

DRINKSTONE – SCHOOL & VILLAGE
A Suffolk History

Published November 2005

DRINKSTONE REVISITED
More stories from a Suffolk Village

Published March 2007

A ZEST FOR LIFE
Biography of economist David B. Jones
told in Letters

Published November 2008

ONE FAMILY'S WAR
A History of one family's experiences in
World War II

Published September 2009

MURDER IN MEADOWFORD MAGNA
A short comedy murder play set in
1920s Suffolk, England

Published February 2010

MISCHIEF IN MEADOWFORD
Another comedy play set in the same
fictional Suffolk village, 1927

Published February 2010

ESTANCIA LAS CORTADERAS
Saga of a family and a farm

Published August 2010

COMING THROUGH - THE LONG JOURNEY
The story of Ruth Minns and Henry Gobbitt,
married in Bredfield, Suffolk, in 1898

Published December 2011

The
Meadowford Mysteries
- Book One

After the Garden Party & Mischief in Meadowford

Sheila Wright

authorHOUSE®

AuthorHouse™
1663 Liberty Drive
Bloomington, IN 47403
www.authorhouse.com
Phone: 1-800-839-8640

Published by AuthorHouse   07/10/2012

ISBN: 978-1-4685-8601-5 (sc)
ISBN: 978-1-4685-8602-2 (hc)
ISBN: 978-1-4685-8616-9 (e)

Telephone 01449 766392
E-mail – sheronkis@hotmail.co.uk
www.kisumubooks.co.uk

This book is printed on acid-free paper.

Cover design by Paul Chilvers www.paulchilvers.co.uk

Contents

Rosanna Ponsonby receives a sinister note-

I am not a patient man. You owe me 50 guineas. Next one, same time, same place. No note this time ... else your ...

What does it mean? Find out as you observe the surprising goings-on in this sleepy Suffolk village in the 1920's....

AFTER THE GARDEN PARTY

ONE – THE GARDEN PARTY

At the clothes stall, Dora Brown shrank under the pitiless gaze of Lady Imogen – why did that lady always make Dora feel she might have gravy stains all down her dress? Nervously, Dora glanced down at herself. Reassured, she selected a green hat adorned with something resembling a dead hen, and placed it on her head.

From behind the stall, Imogen regarded her thoughtfully. 'Why yes, Mrs. Brown', she gushed, 'that hat's perfect for you, really quite charming!'

Blushing hotly, Dora replied 'Do yer really think so, yer ladyship?' Her poor feet ached, her dress stuck to her skin. This sweltering Saturday afternoon was surely the hottest yet of summer 1923.

The dead eye of the fox-fur embellishing Lady Imogen's neck seemed to glint balefully at Dora. Dora worried about her own appearance – she really must find something new for her daughter's wedding.

''Ow much do yer want fer the 'at, m'lady?' she asked. 'Will thruppence do?'

How much did the poor thing have? wondered Lady Imogen.

'Well – you couldn't rise to sixpence maybe, could you?' she answered, 'since it's for the church, you know'.

'That I can't, m'lady', stammered Dora. 'My Charlie's been laid orf since April and you wun't believe the appetites my Tom and the others 'as on 'em'.

Lady Imogen sighed. Trying to look sympathetic, she accepted Dora's coppers. What a way to pass a steamy afternoon! she thought, as she watched her husband John giving the villagers a wide berth, on the far side of the lawn.

With relief, Sir John had spotted his old friend Colonel Mortimer Blunkett and his eccentric Aunt-in-law Maude. The two were reclining in comfy deckchairs shaded by an ancient oak. He sank gratefully into the faded canvas of an empty chair beside the Colonel, mopping his brow.

'Capital weather, what! Sun makes all the difference!' Sir John remarked amiably.

'Thank the Lord for that, old chap', responded Mortimer, removing his favourite rosewood pipe from his lips.. 'Celia's been in a shocking state all week. Tried to make everyone promise to turn up even if it's raining cats and dogs like last year.'

'Might be lucky this time if the thunder keeps away.' Sir John glanced up at some ominously dark clouds.

'Be glad when it's all over. House was in chaos, y'know', rejoined Mortimer. Aunt Maude caressed her little dog's rough coat as she concurred with some force.

'Total chaos! Had to escape with the dogs – my Dotty, and Celia's Gingernuts. Frightful mess everywhere, heaps of old clothes to sort and I swear there were fleas on some of the rubbish'. Maude's voice rose in indignation. 'Celia had the cheek to blame my poor little Dot! I ask you! I shampoo her every Friday, hair's as soft as silk. I told Celia, the wretched things are coming out of that smelly heap you're calling 'Nearly New'. She got my back up. So off we went over the meadow, didn't we, Dotty darling?'

Colonel Mortimer raised his bushy white brows. He frowned at his wife's diminutive Aunt.

'Oh, so it was YOUR fault, Maudie! Couldn't think why Celia was so sharp with me! I was wrong just for breathing! I grabbed my pipe and my paper and sneaked off to the summer house for a bit of peace.'

Sensing criticism of her beloved mistress, Dotty jumped onto Maude's lap and licked her vigorously.

'I did my bit, y' know,' said Maude defensively. 'I washed those hideous vases and china dogs for the White Elephant stall!'

'Talking about white elephants, Maudie', broke in Sir John, 'I couldn't believe my eyes when I spotted that stuffed elephant's foot on the stall!'

'Oh, that old relic!' replied the Colonel. 'It was ours, don't y'know. Given to me and the wife when we left India. Celia never could stand it. We kept it hidden in a cupboard. Moths got it in the end.'

Maude snorted contemptuously. 'They're welcome, if you ask me!'

In the tea tent near the house, Phoebe Jones the doctor's wife set out more cups and saucers. Glancing at her companion Rosanna, she thought her unusually listless.

'Rosanna dear', said Phoebe, 'could you set out some more scones - dab some strawberry jam on them please - while I pop indoors for more milk?'

Hands seemed to reach out towards Rosanna faster than she could cope… pouring tea, taking money, finding change… her head was spinning. Oh no, here was that repulsive Podsfoot man leering at her again.

'Two sugars please, Mrs. Ponsonby, and a slice of date and walnut with the tea.' Podsfoot thrust his face unpleasantly near. His eyes clearly showed insolence and Rosanna shuddered.

'That's five pence please, Mr. Podsfoot.' said Rosanna in a subdued voice as she shakily passed him the plate and cup. Podsfoot placed a folded scrap of paper on the table, saying 'Keep the change, Madam' as he sauntered off.

Rosanna picked up the paper, opened it and popped the sixpence into the money tin. Turning her back on her customers she rapidly smoothed the paper and took a quick look before stuffing it into her jacket pocket. She seemed near to tears; hot tea slopped into saucers as she continued to serve and several recipients glanced at her with curiosity. Podsfoot meanwhile strolled across the lawn towards the group of deckchairs, noisily slurping his tea before dumping cup, saucer and plate on the grass near them and slouching off through the trees. Colonel Mortimer watched him go with obvious distaste.

'Rum chap, that Podsfoot fellow, eh, John. Can't figure him out. How he makes a living from that poky little shop I can't imagine!' remarked the Colonel.

'Shop's closed half the time anyway', said Maude.

Sir John smiled ruefully as he said 'Oh, I've got an idea where his money comes from, though I don't like to talk about it. Don't want the wife to find out, y'know. I made a bit of a bloomer there.'

This interesting exchange was interrupted by the stumbling arrival of Rev. Bertram Valentine, the Vicar. With difficulty, he was carrying an awkward object concealed under his tweed jacket. This he dumped on the grass with obvious relief before breezily greeting his parishioners - 'Wonderful fund-raiser, jolly good show, what!'

Little Dot leaped off Maude's lap to sniff around the object with enthusiasm. The Colonel and Sir John stared open-mouthed as Maude spoke with uncharacteristic tact. 'Vicar! I see you've got yourself a bargain!'

They all found their vague, high-minded priest endearing and no-one wished to question his judgement. Sir John was next to comment with the words 'You've certainly got an eye for the unusual, Vicar!'

'Yes,' beamed Rev. Bertram, 'Awfully striking, isn't it? I thought it would make a perfect birthday gift for Dorothy – something different, you know. Not the usual perfume, or silk stockings, or flowers and chocolates. Something with a bit of character, y'know. So I snapped up this rather esoteric object. Trouble is, it's so heavy.'

Sir John spoke cautiously. 'I do believe it's supposed to be an umbrella stand. They make them in India – one elephant, four useful umbrella stands! Quite a good wheeze I suppose, Bertram – if you like that sort of thing.'

As Dotty moved in a way suggesting she was about to mark the elephant's foot in the time-honoured manner of dogs, Maude hastily snatched her up in her arms. The Vicar continued to beam. 'Dorothy has a wonderful way with arranging all our bits and pieces, you know. She'll find just the place for it in the Vicarage'.

'Indeed she will,' said Maude, 'Dorothy will hardly believe her eyes. But you'll need an awfully big piece of wrapping paper, it's very big and knobbly, Vicar'.

'That's true, dear lady, you might say my present will present a certain problem!' Bertram smiled proudly at his little joke, then continued 'But I'm sure our Ruby will make a fine job of wrapping it, she's a willing little thing. Meanwhile … I think I'll hide it in these bushes for the moment, time I went back to the junketings. Don't want to spoil Dorothy's surprise!'

Rev. Bertram weaved his way back to the main crowds, humming happily to himself. The three friends looked after him with amused tolerance. Maude was first to speak.

'I say, poor old Dorothy, what a let-down! She deserves a proper present, not other people's throw-outs. She's run off her feet living in that big cold house with only that half-witted girl Ruby to help her, y'know.'

'Yes, Bertram's a dear chap,' said Sir John, 'but possibly a bit lacking in imagination. Dorothy has her work cut out helping him, she's a good old stick.'

Maude nodded her head in agreement. 'I must say, I thought poor Dorothy looked exhausted in church last Sunday. I was sitting behind her and I'll swear she fell asleep in the sermon. Her head sort of flopped forward, and I thought, my God, I hope she won't start snoring!'

The friends' peaceful ruminations were rudely interrupted by the shrill voice of Celia, wife of the Colonel. Celia almost ran towards the deck chairs, awkward in her smart high-heels and red-faced with the heat. She was obviously in her most bossy mood. Mortimer sighed deeply.

'Mortimer!' shrieked Celia, 'I thought I told you to help Albert with the bowling! He's got nobody to keep the scores! How will we know who's won the pig if nobody writes down the scores? Can't I trust you to do anything?'

The Colonel jumped up as if shot, knocking over his glass of cider.

'So sorry, m'dear! I just felt a bit shaky on the old pins and had a little sit-down. It's all go at these dos, isn't it?' Reluctantly, he tapped out his comforting pipe and tucked it into his breast pocket, ready for action.

Celia's reply held a note of sarcasm. 'Well, it's all go for some of us, I know that only too well! But I can't run the whole show on my own. I RELY on you, Mortimer!'

'Yes dear, coming, dear, just give me a moment…' Turning out his pockets, the Colonel discovered a notepad and a stub of pencil and followed his irate wife back towards the crowd.

4

At the tea tent, things were no better for Rosanna, her willowy form seeming almost lifeless as she leaned back in a basket chair, preoccupied and pale. Dorothy and Phoebe looked flustered as they tried in vain to keep up the flow of teas and soft drinks, date and walnut cake, cheese scones and all the other donated goodies. When Dorothy returned to the kitchen of The Gables staggering under the weight of a tray of dirties, Phoebe turned to her friend in exasperation. 'Rosanna, come on – I can't manage everything on my own, you know!'

Rosanna's pretty face crumpled. Wearily, she pushed a damp blond wisp of hair back under her hat. 'I'm sorry, Phoebe, honestly I am. It's just that I'm not... not feeling too well.'

Phoebe's tone softened. 'Yes, dear, you do look a bit pale... I expect it's the heat. Look, take off your jacket, let the air get to you.'

Phoebe carefully folded the smart pale blue linen garment and placed it on a chair. Looking around, she saw Maude approaching. Here was a pair of helping hands, however clumsy.

'Maudie!' she called, 'Have you got a moment? Give me a hand with the teas, will you? Dorothy's in the house, and Rosanna here's a bit on the queasy side. Must be the heat getting to her.'

Maude plodded over. She piled up plates, putting various half-eaten buns down on the grass for Dotty to enjoy. Glancing back at those relaxing deck chairs, she noticed the sleek figure of Gerald Ponsonby, Rosanna's husband, resplendent in white flannels, striped blazer and silk cravat, settling into the chair she had left. 'Lucky man!' Maude muttered to herself. Sir John had a fine excuse - gammy leg from a war wound. But Gerald – well, he was dapper as a butterfly, still slender and youthful in appearance despite all those years in India. She guessed the two were exchanging memories of their colonial experiences, Gerald as a State Administrator in the Murree Hills, and Sir John on his family's huge tea plantation in Kenya. Ah, those were the days!

Rev. Bertram had been dutifully moving from stall to stall, encouraging, smiling, uttering mild words of friendship. 'How odd!' thought Maude, 'Why on earth is the Vicar carrying that old sack?' There was something strangely underhand about the way the Vicar now sidled over to the group of deck chairs, where he could be seen surreptitiously poking about in the bushes. Then Gerald took charge of the sack, manhandling it as though the weight was considerable and shoving it under a chair, before the three abandoned their peaceful retreat to the threatening thundery heat and strolled over to the tea tent.

Celia, in her element, wasted no time in setting the new volunteers to work, ringing her bell imperiously to draw the crowd together for the announcement of winners and presentation of prizes. Storm clouds blocked out the sun as a swarm of excited villagers filled the tea tent, and Maude found herself in great demand. How her arms ached! Lady Imogen marshalled helpers to pack unsold clothing into boxes. Summer-house and potting shed were invaded to store items 'for the next jumble sale'.

Sheets of rain began to sweep across the lawns, sending everyone scurrying for their homes. With a sigh of relief, Dorothy, Phoebe and Maude began to pile crockery on trays, while village children with sticky fingers begged the left-overs, stuffing their faces with jam scones and cakes. Dorothy gave Rosanna a basket of china to carry to the house. Still abstracted and miserable, Rosanna complied.

Maude called for her soul-mate Dotty, who seemed to have vanished. 'Dotty! Dotty! Where is the little blighter, she hates thunder!' cried Maude in her best fog-horn voice. Eventually, with a wild yapping, the small bundle of white fur materialised, running in wild circles. Maude became aware of a commotion ahead, as a thin wailing filled the air. Rounding the rhododendrons, she came upon a pathetic sight. Rosanna lay in an awkward damp heap upon the grass, her friends clucking over her. Phoebe seemed to be gently inspecting Rosanna's left foot. 'It's swelling already, you poor dear,' she said. 'Come on Dorothy, help me get poor Rosanna into the house. She tripped over Maude's dratted dog. She was circling like a mad thing.'

Abashed, Maude drew Dotty back into the shade of the rhododendrons.

TWO – SATURDAY EVENING

The rain was slackening off and a yellowish evening light began to creep into the drawing room of The Grange, home of the Ponsonbys. Rosanna lay, still sobbing weakly, on a blue velvet chaise longue and would not be comforted. Phoebe was becoming exasperated. Really, the woman was no better than a hysterical child, what a fuss! Phoebe's husband Walter had given Rosanna a thoroughly professional check and had prescribed cold compresses, warm sweet tea and aspirin. He had then cheerily departed, suggesting a day or two of bed-rest. There was nothing Phoebe wanted more than to go home and join him. It had been an exhausting day. But where was Gerald? He was normally a most attentive husband, but was nowhere to be seen.

Phoebe's bedside manner was wearing thin. 'There, there, dear, do cheer up! You heard what Walter said, just a small sprain. You'll be as right as rain in a day or two!'

Rosanna's voice came weakly through muffled sobs. 'But… there are things I need to do… important things. I must get up. Where is my jacket?'

'Your jacket?' replied Phoebe in puzzlement. 'Well, it can't be far away, it will turn up.' Why was her friend going on about her jacket? The bigger mystery was surely, where was Gerald! Phoebe was mystified.

'Have another little drink, dear – where are those smelling salts? They're just the thing to pick you up. Or how about another little glass of brandy?'

Phoebe placed the brandy glass on the occasional table. She tucked a rug around Rosanna's shaking body. Now the thunder had cleared the air, an evening chill was creeping into the room.

'Phoebe,' asked Rosanna in a pitiful voice, 'do you think you could look in the little cabinet to the left of the fireplace there – that's the one, thank you – and find me some of Gerald's cigarettes, and some matches, please? And there's an ash tray - on that little table by the window. A cigarette might just relax me a bit.'

Phoebe's mouth set in a disapproving line. She knew Gerald disliked his wife's tendency to enjoy a cigarette from time to time. Such an unladylike habit, and bad for the health, her husband Walter always said. But seeing the yearning on her friend's pale ashen face, what could she do but comply?

For at least the tenth time, Phoebe walked into the front hall, to look down the drive for signs of Gerald's return. Re-entering the drawing room she discovered Rosanna shakily trying to stand, her face contorted with pain.

'There's a walking cane in the hall, Phoebe, can you fetch it please? I do need to find my jacket, I must find it!'

'You heard what Walter said, Rosanna – keep off the leg for two or three days at least!' snapped Phoebe. Really, her friend was no better than a spoiled child!

Rosanna sank back and turned her face away. 'Well, if you won't help me, just leave me, for goodness sake!' The words were said wildly, through tears.

Phoebe was intensely relieved at last to hear the front door opening. Gerald! He could look after his pathetic wife himself, and she could leave this madhouse!

Looking towards the door, Phoebe was shocked by Gerald's appearance. He was soaking wet and streaked with mud, in torn shirt sleeves. Gone were his cravat and smart blazer. He was without shoes. His normally immaculate hair was wildly awry and there was a frank desperation about his features. Ignoring Phoebe he fell upon his knees by his wife, caressing her, asking what happened, and finally sinking down, his head in his hands.

Transfixed by the drama, Phoebe stood rigid. Mumbled words reached her ears.

'What's to become of us, my darling? Do you still love me? What went wrong? I can't bear it, it's the end of everything...'

Feeling like a guilty eavesdropper, her brain in a whirl, Phoebe silently tiptoed to the door and let herself out of the house.

THREE – SUNDAY AFTERNOON

Dorothy and Celia had both attended church and had listened dutifully to Rev. Bertram's uplifting words. Both had decided the afternoon was the right moment for visiting the sick. Both had been nonplussed by their reception in the drawing room of The Grange. Now they were in the lane, comparing notes on their friend's condition in hushed but animated voices.

Dorothy spoke confidentially. 'Yes, it was just the same when I visited her! I thought, it's the least I can do, with dear Gerald and Rosanna such close neighbours of ours, and always so supportive to Bertram in his work. Always in their pew on a Sunday, always the first to offer help. But when I called today, Rosanna was distraught! And Gerald, well, nowhere to be seen! When he didn't come to Mattins, I assumed he was at home by Rosanna's bedside, taking care of her.'

'My experience exactly!' replied Celia. A flush of excitement appeared on her neck, finally reaching her cheeks. 'When I called, Gerald was nowhere to be seen. The house was in utter chaos! All Rosanna's jewellery tipped over the floor, and she down on her hands and knees in floods of tears, picking up one piece after another! She was quite unable to hold a conversation!'

Dorothy said thoughtfully 'It was very hot yesterday. Rosanna always suffers from the heat. You don't suppose it's a touch of the sun, do you?'

Celia leant nearer to her friend and lowered her voice discreetly. 'Well, just between you, me, and the gatepost, my dear, I'd say more likely it was too much drink! I don't like to talk about it…. but the room stank of alcohol! I noticed an empty bottle of brandy, and another big bottle, just a tiny drop of whisky left in it, tucked under a corner of Rosanna's rug. There was more than one glass lying around. And they had not been used for water, I assure you!'

Dorothy's eyebrows rose in horror. 'Shocking! On a Sunday afternoon too! I just didn't know what to say to her. Everything I said brought floods of tears.'

Celia made a suggestion. 'Do you think we should have a word with Dr. Jones? Or maybe with the dear Vicar, of course?'

Dorothy's voice hardened. 'Dear Vicar isn't exactly what I'd call my husband just at the moment. He's behaving very oddly. I had to call him three times for lunch, and when he finally came he was covered in dust and cobwebs! Said he'd lost something, wouldn't say what. I believe he'd been in the garden shed. That's Charlie Brown's domain normally. It's where we keep the lawn mower, you know.'

'Extraordinary!' responded Celia.

Further grievances poured from Dorothy and her voice took on a martyred tone. 'And when Bertram finally came in, he was quite testy with me. Said it was a fine thing when a man couldn't take a stroll in his own garden without being cross-questioned!'

'Oh dear!' murmured Celia, who had rarely seen Dorothy so upset. Dorothy surreptitiously wiped away a tear before continuing her tale of woe.

'And I was thinking, it's a fine state of affairs when a wife tries so hard to be organised... and on a Sunday too, it's Ruby's day off... and her husband can't even be bothered to be punctual at mealtimes! You know how greasy roast lamb becomes when it's cold!'

Celia tried to soothe her. 'Oh I do sympathise, dear. These men are so thoughtless.'

An unmistakeable voice caused the two ladies to pause and gaze down the lane, where a red-faced Maude soon came stomping into view in her muddy brogues and usual tweedy ensemble.

'Dotty! Dotty! Come here, you naughty dog!' Seeing her two friends she explained 'That dratted dog's gone off again, I don't know what's got into her! I meant to visit poor Rosanna this afternoon. I feel I must, since it was my Dotty who caused her fall!' She stopped to catch her breath.

'Just how I feel, Maudie,' said Celia. 'Since Rosanna was in my garden when she hurt herself, I feel responsible somehow.'

Maude obviously had more news to impart and carried on in scandalised tones. 'Funny thing. I just met Gerald near the churchyard. Although I noticed he wasn't at the service this morning, was he! But it was most peculiar. He seemed to be carrying a pail of soapy water! He tried to hide it when he saw me, holding it behind his legs. He looked most distracted and wild. I thought he must be worried about his poor wife, but when I asked should I call on her, he was most evasive!'

'How strange!' said Dorothy. 'They do both seem most terribly upset.'
Celia agreed. 'Yes, exactly. Frightfully upset, both of them. Maybe we should try calling again tomorrow morning, give them time to collect themselves. Well Maudie, good luck finding your dog.'

Maude plodded off, her calls of 'Dotty, Dotty' disturbing the Sunday peace of the village.

'Whatever could Gerald be doing with soapy water in the churchyard?' mused Dorothy. Celia had no answer.

'Search me. Seems everyone's lost their senses. Maudie's quite dotty herself these days, isn't she, Dorothy? They do say dogs become like their owners. In this case I think the owner is getting more and more like her dog. But I suppose we should make allowances for age. She's my mother's sister, you know, and mother was quite crazy by the time she passed away, poor dear!'

Dorothy glanced at her watch before replying 'Oh dear, how sad. Well, Celia, I must get home, it's nearly time for Evensong. I'll see you tomorrow.'

The two friends said their farewells and parted, each wondering what further bizarre behaviour the morrow might bring.

That evening, in the middle Drift Cottage, Dora Brown was tidying her kitchen, sweeping mud off the red brick floor before settling down for a snooze by the range. The door opened abruptly and in strolled her son Tom. 'Hi, Ma!' he said, casually kicking off his boots and plonking himself down on the old settle, where the aged dog obligingly made room for him. Small pieces of leaf and twig fell from his clothes as he moved.

'Where on earth you been, young man?' asked his mother.

'Oh…. Jus' out and about!' Tom replied evasively.

'But you'm missed yer dinner! What got into yer, boy? 'Ere yer come 'ome, empty 'anded, an' not a word about where you bin all day!'

Tom began busily investigating the pockets of his ancient jacket.

'Not empty 'anded, Ma. Look, I got carrots, and turnips. I 'ad spuds too, but I got 'ungry and 'et 'em.' He placed his haul proudly on an old newspaper beside him.

'You 'et 'em? Raw spuds? Yer mad, boy! Don't blame me if yer gets the runs! Can't eat spuds raw, them's poison!' exclaimed his mother.

'Oo said nuthin' about eatin' 'em raw?' replied Tom. 'I ain't stupid, I cooked 'em!'

'Cooked 'em! Don't you be fibbin' to me, my lad!' said Dora.

'No, honest!' said Tom, his eyes wide with injured innocence. 'I were down in the woods near the church. All me snares from Saturd'y was empty, not a rabbit nor a pheasant in 'em. So I stuffed me pockets full o' veggies from Squire's plot. His gardener's never workin' there of a Sunday. I got 'em fer you an' the kids.'

'Yer a rascal, Tom,' replied Dora, mollified. 'I don't s'pose they'll miss just a 'andful. But 'ow did yer cook them spuds?'

'Well, it were rum,' began Tom. 'I smells burnin'. So I follows me nose, into that spinney be'ind the shops. There among the brambles I finds a great 'eap of ashes. Still a-smoulderin', they was. I pokes about with me stick to stir up a flame. In the middle I sees an 'unk o' metal, like the bottom of a pan only thicker. So I thinks to meself, them ashes is glowin', I've got spuds in me pocket and a rumble in me tum, an' 'ere's a ready-made griddle fer the cookin'! So I sets me down comfy like, an' waits!'

'An' I were worryin' me 'ead about you going 'ungry all day!' said Dora.

Tom continued. 'I put on some dry twigs to keep things a-goin'. I could tell by the smell when they was ready. By, there was some rum ol' smells around that place! Like when yer burns old boots, it were. An' another smell! Paraffin!'

'Well, yer a rascal! I'll give yer old boots 'n' paraffin! Yer Dad needed yer 'ere, to 'elp fix the old sty for that there piglet. Still you done good fer us all, winnin' the bowlin' yesterd'y, so I can't get riled. Can't be bad, a fine young piglet down the garden, and you brung us carrots an' turnips. Shame about the spuds, though.'

Dora settled her aching back against the cushions and beamed at her son.

'Tomorrer's a good day, anyways. Monday. That's when yer Dad mows the Vicar's lawn and the churchyard. That Vicar, 'e's a good man, and 'e pays 'an'some, so I wun't grumble.'

'Don't ferget, Ma, I got a day's work too. It'll be 'oeing again, turnips or mangolds, at Long Abbeyfield. That's a mucky job, it's all clay over there. I starts at six. Well, I'll go and 'ave a look at me little pig, see 'ow 'e's settlin' in!'

And with that, Tom was out of the door whistling, leaving his weary mother to count her blessings by her fireside and await Charlie's return from the 'Cat and Feathers'.

FOUR – MONDAY MORNING

Monday morning found Rosanna still abandoned to despair in the elegant drawing room at The Grange. Gerald drew back the grey-blue drapes framing the tall sash windows, each with their wide white-painted window seat below, and folding shutters at the sides. Not much light entered; it was a dreary day. Gerald was still pale, as if in shock, his hair unkempt. Protruding from the right sleeve of his jacket was a bloodstained handkerchief, roughly knotted around his wrist. He turned wearily to look at his wife. There she lay, face turned away from the light, emitting tiny moans and groans. She seemed to have totally given up on life.

'Come on, Rosanna old girl! Talk to me! Tell me what's wrong, please!' he pleaded.

'I'm so frightened, Gerald! You haven't seen Mr. Podsfoot today, have you?' Gerald jumped nervously and seemed to turn a shade paler.

'Podsfoot? Podsfoot? No, why should I see him?' He knelt beside his wife, taking her limp hand in his.

'Oh…. I don't know, I just keep imagining things.' Rosanna started to sob quietly. 'I feel as if it's all over, Gerald! It's all hopeless!'

'What's all over, my darling? You know I love you, I've always loved you, and we've still got each other.' Gerald spoke with desperation. 'Please let me see you smile!'

Rosanna tried, but failed to do more than grimace painfully. 'Why are you so kind to me, Gerald? I don't deserve it, I feel as if I've spoilt everything!' she wailed.

'But darling! You have been happy with me most of the time, haven't you? I know, in India, there were times when I was too busy to spend much time with you, and I know you were dreadfully homesick. But that's years ago now! We've been so happy these last years…. haven't we?'

Rosanna gazed fondly at her husband before answering 'Yes, yes, it's been so jolly living here. Until…. until…' Her words trailed into silence.

'Until what, my dearest?'
Rosanna suddenly noticed his bandaged arm. 'You're bleeding, Gerald! What happened to your arm?'

Gerald tugged at the sleeve, trying to cover the bloodstained hanky. 'Oh, that … it's nothing, really. Just some brambles got me in the garden this morning. Why don't you try and get some sleep, dear? Have a little drink, then see if you can nod off.'

'I might, if you could just stay with me for a while, Gerald. Sit in the armchair and have a little doze yourself. You seem to have been popping in and out of the house non-stop these last few days. I need you here, with me.'

'Yes, sorry, darling. Things to do around the place, you know. All right, I'll sit here, and we'll try and get a little peace, before…. before…'

'Before what, Gerald?'

'Oh, before lunch time, I suppose. Mabel's here, she's busy in the kitchen. I think she's making us a ham salad. Now, please can we just try to relax in peace and quiet. I promise I won't go out again.'

As he finished speaking, the shrill tones of the phone in the hall could be heard. Looking uneasy, Gerald got to his feet. 'I'd better go and answer the phone, dear. I'll come straight back.' He disappeared into the hall, returning moments later, tense and preoccupied. Wordlessly he sank into the cushioned chair, where he sat gazing at the flowered carpet.

'Who was on the phone, Gerald?' asked Rosanna. Her husband answered with reluctance, not meeting her tear-filled eyes.

'Oh… it was the Vicar. Nothing important. He asked if I could go over to the Vicarage, but I told him, sorry, I can't, it's my duty to stay with my wife who has a badly sprained ankle. I promise I'll stay with you, dearest.'

'Thank you, Gerald,' whispered his wife. 'But I'm still so worried about my jacket. Have you seen it anywhere?'

Gerald reassured his wife that as soon as she was well again, he would take her to London on a day-return, and together they would select the most beautiful jacket – or even an entire new two-piece – in Harrods. 'Never mind that old jacket,' he said, 'only one thing matters to me. Look at me, darling, and tell me honestly, do you still love me?'

Rosanna turned her troubled countenance towards her husband. 'Gerald, why do you keep asking me? You know I love you. Truly, I do.'

Gazing into the sky blue eyes of his wife, Gerald was sure he could detect a look of desperation, almost of rank terror. He lowered his own gaze, wondering what emotions his own eyes revealed. Rosanna put out a shaking hand and took a cigarette from the near-empty packet beside her. Gerald silently lit Rosanna's cigarette and took one himself. What a state they were both in! he thought. Sighing deeply, he took his wife's hand in his own, and the two commenced a silent vigil. An atmosphere of foreboding filled the usually charming room.

Down the lane in the leafy garden of The Old Hall, family home of Lady Imogen and Sir John Greenleaf, all was timeless and peaceful. Sir John, legs akimbo and leaning on his cane, stood in deep conversation with the Colonel. Both had well-loved ancient pipes in the corners of their mouths. Amid the odour of top-quality tobacco, the scent of old-fashioned pinks and rambling roses wafted around the two elderly gentlemen. Behind them loomed the ancient Hall, its oaken timbers seeming to lean at all angles. It had withstood four hundred years of wild weather and looked likely to survive for at least four hundred more. The clay lump between the oaks was painted a sunny orange-pink, a delightful contrast to the green of the sheltering trees. This homestead was Sir John's haven and delight.

Sir John looked bemused as he listened to the Colonel's news. 'So, you say Podsfoot's shop is shut up. Funny that, he's always open on Mondays, even if he has a couple of days off later in the week,' said Sir John.

'Yes, it's annoying really,' answered the Colonel. 'I wanted to take back a statuette I bought there last week. Labelled 'solid bronze', it was, and had a price to match. When I got it home, Maudie didn't half pull my leg about it. Seems it's nothing but papier maché moulded around a stone to give weight, with a few layers of cheap metal and varnish on top. That's what Maude reckons. I feel a bit of a fool, to tell the truth, old boy.'

'Is that so?' responded Sir John. 'Well, you're not the only old fool around here, I'm afraid! I'll tell you now, if you'll swear to keep it to yourself. Podsfoot swindled me good and proper too. I bought an oil painting in his shop. It was a woodland scene, very detailed, with a clear signature, 'Thomas Gainsborough'. I won't tell you what I paid for it. It hurts me now just thinking about it. But Podsfoot was new to the village then. I should have checked out his credentials first, I suppose. I really believed it was a Gainsborough, and I gave it to Imogen last Christmas, and she's extremely proud of it.'

'I know the one,' said the Colonel. 'It hangs in your front hall.'

'That's right. Old Maudie, you know, she may be half crazy but she's got a head full of knowledge on her. Of course she worked in the Archives at the National Gallery before the War. She came to me quietly and told me she had her doubts.'

'Did she now?' said the Colonel. 'She's a dark horse! She never said anything to me and Celia!'

'Well, she's a good old girl and she knew how highly Imogen prized my gift. She didn't want to spoil things. She contacted an old friend of hers, an art expert from Sothebys, and he popped up one weekend while Imogen was in London on a shopping spree. Maude was right – it's a fake. What a fool I felt!'

'Easily done, old chum,' said the Colonel heartily, feeling much better now about his own gullibility. 'Does Imogen know?'

'Thankfully, no. She'd never let me forget it if she knew the truth. Besides, she's always boasting to her friends about owning a genuine Gainsborough. So I'm stuck with it. Of course I went round and tackled Podsfoot and he was most unpleasant. He openly sneered at me, told me it was my job, not his, to verify an article. He said any object is worth whatever any old fool will pay for it, as far as he can see!'

'Hard luck!' said the Colonel. 'That man's made idiots of both of us! Of course I won't tell a soul, John. But it makes me mad when he sails past me in that new Wolseley of his, giving himself airs. All based on sharp practice and swindles. Funny thing - I never took to him from the first. He reminded me of someone else, years ago in India. Can't quite picture who, though.'

'It's a pity he ever came here,' replied Sir John, with some rancour. 'Spoils the village atmosphere when you can't trust your own neighbours.'

The two old friends' confidences were interrupted by the breathless arrival on the scene of Aunt Maude. She addressed a torrent of words towards the hapless Colonel.

'Have you seen that dog of mine, Mortimer? I don't know what's got into her lately. Won't come when I call her, goes mad for no reason at all. After the garden party she just took off, terrified by the thunder. I finally found her by following her yapping. There she was, barking her silly head off at that old scarecrow in Jack Draper's beanfield by the church. Barking like a mad thing! It was the dickens of a job to call her off. Same thing happened yesterday. Crossed the churchyard, and she was over the wall and careering down there to bark at that scarecrow! Nosing all round it, trying to dig, and taking not a blind bit of notice of me. Honestly! I'm not as young as I was. I can't go careering all over the countryside chasing her!'

She finally paused for breath and the Colonel sighed wearily.

'Righto, Maudie, I'll come along with you. Between us we'll find her.' He turned to Sir John in farewell and that gentleman rewarded him with a conspiratorial wink in sympathy.

No sooner was Sir John alone than he heard his name being called, frantically, from the direction of the house. Lady Imogen almost ran towards her husband, seizing him by the arm without any of her usual composure.

'John! Come indoors! Terrible news, terrible!' She half dragged him towards the house, gasping as if in shock. Sir John's gammy leg was giving him jip. He tried to calm her, and slow her down. 'Take it easy, old girl! Whatever is the matter?'

'It's just too, too dreadful, John!' Her words tumbled over each other in a mixture of horror and exhilaration. 'The Vicar rang, he wants us to go over to the Vicarage straight away!'

'Well, that's not too terrible, we'll go and have a pleasant chat, shall we? I expect he wants to discuss the PCC meeting,' said Sir John soothingly.

'No…..Listen! You don't understand! He sounded upset on the phone. He… he said something about a body in his cellar!' Lady Imogen finally got the shocking words out.

Sir John stopped short. 'What! No, you must have misunderstood him, Imogen. He can't have said that.' His words had little effect on his wife.

'He was quite clear, John. A little shaken, but clear. He wants us there now. He said Dorothy's beside herself, and their Ruby's in hysterics. It was Ruby who found it. She went down into the cellar to tidy up, after the coalman delivered a couple of tons this morning. You know, there's a chute you can see, in their back courtyard. The coal cart tips the stuff straight down the chute into the cellar. Dorothy sent Ruby down to tidy the heap with a stiff brush. She came rushing back up the stairs screaming that there was a man's leg sticking out from under the coal!'

'A man's leg?' repeated Sir John. 'Surely not! Maybe it was just an old shoe down there?'

Lady Imogen's voice rose to a shrill squeal. 'No, it's true. The Vicar's in a state. He said he went down himself, to investigate, and there's a leg in the shoe! Stiff! Dead, I suppose! He's called the police.'

'Poor chap must be in shock,' said Sir John sombrely. 'Of course I must go over. I'm sure Dorothy would appreciate it if you came too, my dear, if you can face it.'

'Do you really think I should come?' replied Lady Imogen, a trace of eagerness in her voice. 'I wonder if some old tramp fell down that chute in the dark.'

'We'll find out what the police have to say. No time to waste, Imogen, let's toddle over together and see what we can do.'

At the Vicarage, the bell pull in the grey brick porch was answered by a nervous-looking Mabel, who had abandoned her duties in the home of the Ponsonbys at Gerald's suggestion. Not willing to go over there himself, and learning from the Vicar that their maid Ruby had run home, Gerald had told Mabel that Ruby was not feeling well and the Vicar needed extra help. Mabel's curiosity was aroused and she had willingly walked to the Vicarage. Mabel liked to feel useful, and the Ponsonbys seemed to have retreated into a world of their own. She had taken them their tasty lunch of ham salad and had been quite hurt when the two picked listlessly at the food with barely a thank you. They were both behaving so strangely, as if they were in some unhappy dream world where no-one could reach them.

Now Mabel led the Squire and his wife along the dingy book-lined hallway, into Rev. Valentine's large untidy study. The room contained several comfy leather armchairs, inherited by Dorothy from her father, who had been Rural Dean. The familiar smell of dusty old books and papers, plus traces of strong tobacco smoke, filled their nostrils. Dorothy often suspected her husband of entering his beloved study simply to put his feet up and smoke his old briar pipe, when he would tell her he 'must get on with his sermon'. But he was such a benign, kindly man; she could not criticise him for this. Some of the parishioners were unbelievably demanding, and her Bertram deserved his bit of peace.

They were greeted by familiar faces wearing unwonted expressions of solemnity, like mourners at the funeral of a person they had not really liked. To the discerning eye, curiosity and a kind of unholy glee underlaid the assumed seriousness. Reverend Bertram jumped up to greet his neighbours, shaking them warmly by the hand, saying 'Thank you for coming over. I feel so much more at ease now we have some friends around us. Dorothy and I have been somewhat overwhelmed by events.'

Two shabby armchairs were drawn up for the newcomers, who joined the group facing Constable Black. The Constable was holding court at the Vicar's mahogany desk. He had cleared a space so he might jot down every word that was said in his official police notepad. He was glad to see Sir John, who was respected as a wise Magistrate in the local Court.

Really, thought Lady Imogen, the situation recalled uncomfortable girlhood sessions in the headmistress's study, where with other guilty schoolgirls she had sat wriggling nervously and hoping no questions would be directed at her. But why should she feel guilty now? After all, she was only here to help the dear Vicar and Dorothy in very distressing circumstances. She met Dorothy's gaze and did her best to smile warmly as if nothing was wrong. Then she concentrated on calming her thoughts and taking in what was being said.

The Constable spoke with authority. He was obviously in the midst of cross-questioning the Vicar. 'So let's get this straight, Reverend. Tell me again, when did you last see Mr. Podsfoot alive?'

'Did you say, Mr. Podsfoot?' interrupted Sir John. 'What's happened to him?'

The Constable turned towards the Squire, trying to sound suitably deferential. 'Well, you see, Sir John, there has been a very unfortunate accident. Mr. Podsfoot was found dead in the Vicar's cellar this morning, under a heap of newly-delivered coal.'

This statement caused Mabel to screw up her hanky, pressing it to her face to drown her gasps and whimpers of 'Poor Ruby!' Lady Imogen clutched her husband's hand and sat rigid, her eyes staring at the assembled group.

Dorothy's hair was escaping from her hair-grips and was tumbling around her ears, giving her a dishevelled air. She was wringing her hands nervously as she studied her husband's face.

The Constable asked the question again. 'Think carefully, please, Sir. When did you last see him?'

The Vicar hesitated a moment, then said firmly 'It must have been Saturday. Yes, Saturday, at the Church Garden Party, at Colonel Blunkett's, The Gables, you know. Most of the village was there, of course. I'm sure they'll agree that Mr. Podsfoot looked just as he normally looks – detached and unfriendly, but definitely alive and well.'

Sir John interjected 'In fact, I'd say he was looking mighty pleased with himself, quite the cock of the roost.'

Constable Black scribbled in his notebook before looking up to speak.

'So he didn't look unwell at all and was acting as normal? It could have been an accident, maybe. He might have just tumbled down your coal chute in the dark. Was he a drinking man, would you say?'

Sir John answered with conviction. 'Not as far as I know, in fact I'd say he was quite a cool character, kept himself apart. Never knew him to mix much with the locals, I don't think he frequented the 'Cat and Feathers' at all. Not really the chummy type, and of course he doesn't come from round these parts.'

Reverend Valentine concurred, trying to justify the general cool attitude towards Mr. Podsfoot. 'Of course, we try to welcome newcomers, draw them into our little community. But when I visited him to ask if he'd come on our Parochial Church Council, he being a businessman, so to speak, and used to finances, he just didn't want to know. Next time I called, to ask whether he had settled in all right, he more or less shut the door in my face.' His voice betrayed peevish resentment as he continued. 'In fact, I was a little surprised that he even bothered to make an appearance at our Garden Party.'

Observing the nods of agreement around the room, the Constable sensed the general feeling towards the deceased. 'So you wouldn't say he was a popular character in the village, then?'

Many voices were raised, and the dear departed was labelled 'Standoffish', 'Rude and unpleasant', 'Giving himself airs' - all of which opinions were duly recorded in the notebook.

'Hmm, that's interesting. We can't just assume it was an accident, I'm afraid,' said the Constable. 'I phoned the Inspector at Upper Abbeyfield as soon as I got your message about the incident. Maybe I'd better ask you all to stay in this room and wait until he comes.'

'We're not under suspicion, I trust?' asked the Vicar.

'That's not for me to say, Reverend. These things have to be investigated proper. It all takes time, you know. Can't rush it. Can't even move the body yet, might destroy evidence.'

'Oh Bertram!' cried Dorothy, 'how perfectly horrid if that poor dead man has to stay down in our cellar all day!'

The Vicar patted her shoulder tenderly. 'Don't get upset, my dear, we won't be leaving you alone in the house, will we? It's a shame Ruby ran off like that, or I'd get her to make tea for us all while we wait. But the poor girl had a most dreadful shock!'

'Yes, she rushed out of the house in hysterics. I doubt she'll want to come back.' Dorothy produced an embroidered hanky with which to delicately wipe eyes and nose. 'Ruby's a sensitive girl. But Mabel has kindly come over to see if she can help. Mabel, do you think you could find your way around our kitchen and bring us a tray of tea? There are some nice ginger biscuits in the larder, and a caraway seed cake in the big Coronation tin on the middle shelf.'

Mabel rose to do her bidding, but the Constable looked up from his notes to say 'Miss Mabel, I understand you're a close friend of Miss Ruby. There's another job you might do first, to help things along please.'

He turned to Reverend Valentine. 'About Ruby, Sir. You say your maid Ruby found the body. So we'll have to talk to her too. Miss Mabel, do you think you could go to her home and bring her back here? If she won't come, tell her I'll have to come and fetch her, but I really don't have time for that before the Inspector arrives. Tell her there's nothing to worry about but we need to know exactly what occurred.'

Mabel was gratified at finding herself so important to the enquiry. She pulled on her warm jacket and strutted off proudly on her short stubby legs.

The Constable was bristling with importance. 'Now, I need all your names please, and addresses. Then you must each say exactly when you last saw Podsfoot and tell me anything that might pertain to the case. We'll be searching his shop too, to see what clues about his lifestyle we can discover...'

A loud insistent knocking sounded from down the hall. The Constable stood up. 'Stay here, ladies and gentlemen, I'll answer that'. He left the room and soon strident voices were heard approaching. In rushed Colonel Blunkett, followed by his wife's Aunt Maude. Both were flushed and excitable.

Maude's voice rose above the deep drone of the Colonel. 'We heard the Constable was here at the Vicarage so we came straight here! There's been a burglary in the village! I really don't know what things are coming to!'

'Don't get so excited, Maudie old gel!' said the Colonel, laying a restraining hand on her arm. 'It's only a burglary! It's not as if there's been a murder! Just calm down and tell the Constable quietly!'

Maude was unstoppable. Not noticing the meaningful glances exchanged around her, she spoke her piece. 'Listen, all of you! What happened was, Mortimer and I went round to the back of Mr. Podsfoot's antique shop. We were trying to find my Dotty, she's run off again. And guess what, the back window was smashed, glass everywhere!'

The Colonel took over. 'We looked in, of course, just to check everything was all right. And there's the dickens of a mess in there! Papers all over the floor, drawers pulled open....'

'So we went round to the front again and tried the door,' said Maude. 'But Mr. Podsfoot's definitely not there. The shop's all shut up.' She gazed around at her listeners to see what impression her dramatic news had made.

The Constable could keep quiet no longer. He spoke drily with a slightly mocking tone. 'We know Mr. Podsfoot's not there, Madam! Of course he's not in his shop, because he's lying here dead, in the cellar under this very room! Dead men don't open shops, now do they?'

Maude gave a banshee shriek and grabbed onto the Colonel's large bulk. 'Mortimer! I think I'm going to faint! That can't be true.... What, dead in the Vicar's cellar? It's impossible!'

Mortimer put his arm around his small relative for comfort before addressing Constable Black. 'Well, Constable, bless my soul! Can't say I ever liked the man! But dead! And in the Vicar's own home!'

The Reverend spoke somewhat huffily. 'It's no good blaming me! I can't help it if people fall down my coal chute, can I? It's not something you expect, is it?'

Constable Black addressed the assembled company severely. 'It all has to be investigated by the proper procedure, ladies and gentlemen. So like I said, you might all be important witnesses, so you have to stay here and wait. Sit down, Madam, and you too, Colonel Sir. No need to get excited.' He was enjoying directing proceedings. 'When reinforcements come we'll bring in everyone else who might know something. So settle down please, and wait.'

Maude was agitated. 'Dorothy, do you think I might use your phone to tell Celia where we are? And ask her if my Dotty's found her way home yet?'

'Yes, of course you may,' responded Dorothy. Off bustled Maude to the hall, where her loud and animated conversation with her niece could be clearly heard. No-one was surprised when Maude returned to ask the Valentines whether it was acceptable if Celia came to join them all.

'Why not?' said Bertram. 'Celia may have noticed something that the rest of us have missed.'

Dorothy felt it her duty to go to the kitchen, returning with biscuits, seed cake and some rather dry looking cheese sandwiches. Maude put herself in charge of the large brown teapot. The atmosphere became quite convivial, even though the party soon ran out of milk and bread. Whispered conversations were heard, and although no-one was allowed down the taped-off cellar stairs everyone admired the door to the cellar and raised their eyebrows in satisfactory manner.

Bertram and Dorothy began to feel quite people of note. For once, everyone hung on the Vicar's every word!

FIVE – MONDAY AFTERNOON

By mid-afternoon, Inspector Sharpe, Celia, Mabel and Ruby had all arrived. All had noted Inspector Sharpe's impressive car in the driveway. Two plain-clothes detectives and a police doctor, summoned by the Inspector, had arrived and were shown to the notorious cellar door. They had disappeared down the stone steps carrying the tools of their mysterious trades.

Constable Black's yearning for promotion was based on his envy of the Inspector, a man who was given a gleaming automobile for his daily work, while he himself was expected to arrive on the scene of every crime by 'sit-up-and-beg' pedal bike.

The Inspector took immediate charge, greeting everyone, then ousting the Constable from the comfy round-backed chair to take up position behind the desk as main interrogator. He checked through the Constable's careful list of names and addresses, tweaking his fine black waxed moustaches thoughtfully as he perused the account of the case so far. He added the names and addresses of the newcomers. Each person was asked how well they knew Podsfoot, what their impression of his character and lifestyle was, when they had last seen him, and so on. Copious notes were written. Police personnel entered and left the room, and were also heard in the garden, as they went about their work.

The concentration of those in the study began to wander. The Inspector thanked them for their patience, and had particular words of praise for Mabel, who had succeeded in persuading young Ruby to return to the Vicarage. Mabel glowed. She appeared to visibly increase in stature and was doing a magnificent job of consoling Ruby and encouraging her to speak up bravely.

Around four o'clock, with most facts now at his fingertips, the Inspector summed up the investigation so far. Everyone became still and attentive, all eyes were on his face.

'Ladies and gentlemen,' he began, 'thank you for your help with our enquiries. Since this morning there have been certain developments. Dr. Jones and our own police doctor have both examined the body. They agree that Mr. Podsfoot died at least two days ago – that is, on Saturday. The two wounds on his head, one on the forehead and one behind the ear, are severe enough to have bled heavily. His skull is fractured, the wounds are open, and yet there's no pool of blood evident where he was found in the cellar.'

At this, Lady Imogen moaned softly and wailed 'Oh, this is all too upsetting! All this talk about pools of blood....'

The Inspector looked irritated and commented 'Since you are not directly involved in the case and are here only at the request of Reverend and Mrs.

Valentine, Madam, there is no need for you to stay unless you wish to.'

This caused Lady Imogen to sit up smartly, dignified, imperious and attentive. She had no wish to miss any of the unfolding drama, and murmured her apologies.

The Inspector continued. 'What I have to tell you, ladies and gentlemen, is that it's possible Mr. Podsfoot was attacked somewhere else in the vicinity, then his body was dropped down the coal chute some hours later. Some time, obviously, before the coal merchant delivered his load this morning. The coal landed on top of the corpse.'

Everyone gasped and the room fell silent. Finally, Colonel Blunkett spoke.

'Do you think the man was attacked by whoever burgled his shop, Sir? Podsfoot might have disturbed a thief, and got thumped for it!'

The Inspector explained further. 'My colleagues have thoroughly investigated Mr. Podsfoot's shop. The only blood is around the broken window, spattered on the glass, and it's quite fresh, certainly not two days old. Presumably whoever smashed that window was not a practised burglar. There's no sign of blood inside the building. The shop part is untouched, the perpetrator was only interested in the office at the back. It was no ordinary burglary. Whoever broke in was not looking for money or valuables. There's plenty of small stuff in the shop, jewellery and the like, that would have been easy to take. Also, a surprising amount of cash is in the open drawers in the office, big bundles of bank notes. They are still lying there, although the building has been made secure, of course. Someone used force to open the drawers, which were locked. A lot of papers were removed and scattered around, but the money was left.'

Sir John was next to interrupt, highly indignant. 'Indeed! By rights, some of that money's mine!' he declared.

There were gasps all round and his wife exclaimed in a horrified voice 'John, what do you mean?' Surely her respected, aristocratic husband was not involved in this sordid business!

There were more gasps when the Colonel angrily remarked 'Some of that money's mine, too, truth be told!'

The Inspector regarded the two men steadily before saying 'Really, gentlemen? I'll be asking you about that later, in private. Make a note, Constable.'

Constable Black scribbled on his pad. 'Right you are, Sir!'

The Inspector continued. 'Well, to go on with the evidence. There were several bundles of letters, all carefully tied and wrapped in brown paper. They'd been torn open and scattered about. Strangely, none are addressed to Mr. Podsfoot himself. That's being investigated. There are certain inconsistencies, too. The sign on the shop front says 'T. S. Podsfoot, Antiques'. We found invoices made out to 'Mr. Talbot Stanley Podsfoot' – mostly from the local garage, and a few from that new mens' wear shop...'

Here he was interrupted by Sir John, who asked 'Do you mean that new shop at Upper Abbeyfield, Inspector? That's too pricey for me, I'm afraid.'

'That's the one, Sir John', confirmed the Inspector. 'Now, to continue. There were business receipts, of course, in the name Talbot Podsfoot. Also some letters of complaint from customers.' As he said this, his eye rested speculatively first on Sir John, then on the Colonel. Both shifted uncomfortably and looked down, as he continued. 'But curiously, Mr. Podsfoot seems to have changed his name. Quite a few of the earlier letters and documents refer to 'Mr. Stanley Talbot'.

These words had a galvanising effect on the Colonel, who jumped up, amazed. 'By Jingo! Stanley Talbot! That's it, of course! That's what's been bugging me these last few months! Well I'll be jiggered!'

'I gather the name Stanley Talbot means something to you, Sir,' said the Inspector. 'Would you care to explain?'

The Colonel had become quite red in the face, and his bushy white moustache and eyebrows seemed to take on a life of their own, like a family of wriggling caterpillars, as various expressions crossed his face. He finally spoke, slowly but firmly. 'I remember it all now! Every time I saw that wretched man my thoughts went back to those years in India and I didn't know why! Now I remember! I knew the man, in the Madras set-up, twenty-five years ago at least! The name 'Podsfoot' foxed me. He was never Mr. Podsfoot then. He was Stanley Talbot.'

'In what context did you know him, Sir?' enquired the Inspector.

'In a murky context, that's what!' boomed the Colonel. 'Something jolly fishy! Can't remember the details, but Piggy would know!'

Celia leaned forward to ask 'Piggy, did you say, Mortimer?'

'Yes dear, you remember old Piggy! He was my mate in school, then we were at Sandhurst together. Then blow me down if we didn't end up together in Madras! Old Piggy always knew what was going on. Gerald and Rosanna were in Madras too, for a few years, before they came home here. I think Rosanna hated the heat, or the lifestyle, or some such thing. Well I'll be damned!'

The Inspector asked 'Can you give us a contact number for this Mr. Piggy, Sir? Where does he live now? Unusual name, shouldn't be hard to trace!'

The Colonel gave a gruff laugh. 'We called him Piggy at school because ... well.... he was always such a pig! A real greedy guts! Good mate though, great on the rugby field because of his weight. He was really Percival Pratt. We called him Piggy Pratt!'

The Inspector's patience was wearing thin. 'Well, can you give us a phone number for Mr. Pratt, please, Sir?'

'Major Pratt, retired, he is, and he lives at 'The Willows', Little Bumpstead, near Woodbridge. He must be in the book.'

'Constable, make a note of that name and address, please. Phone him and ask about Mr. Stanley Talbot. Look sharp, now!' said the Inspector briskly. The Constable left the room obediently.

'Now', continued the Inspector, 'would anyone else like to share their knowledge of Mr. Podsfoot – I should say Mr. Talbot – and his past history or character?'

There was a murmuring and shaking of heads. Phrases such as 'No-one liked him', 'shady piece of work' reached the Inspector's ears. Mabel tentatively put up her hand, like a child in school.

'Yes, Miss Mabel? You can tell us something?' asked the Inspector hopefully.

Mabel spoke somewhat hesitantly. 'Well, yes….. there was somethin' but I din't like to say before. Don't seem right somehow, tellin'….' She broke off in confusion.

The Inspector assumed his gentlest voice and expression. 'You may be the only person who can carry this investigation forward, Miss Mabel. So please don't be shy.'

'Well, about two weeks ago…… it were a Sat'd'y, I knows that, because I finishes early of a Sat'd'y, at a quarter to four. I was on me way 'ome from The Grange. I thought I'd take a short cut through the churchyard an' I 'eard voices!' She stopped, overcome with nerves.

Reverend Valentine came to her rescue in his kindest voice - the one he reserved for small children or those he took to be of weak intellect.

'There's nothing strange about hearing voices in the churchyard, my girl. People go there all the time, to visit the graves of their dear ones, you know!'

Spoken to in this patronising way, as if she were stupid, strengthened Mabel's resolve to tell all. 'I knows that, Vicar!' she said scornfully. 'I goes too, me Gran's buried there. But what I 'eard as I come round the corner, by them big old yew trees, was a man shoutin'. An' there were a woman cryin'. I couldn't see 'er proper 'cos they was sort of hidden in the trees. But I could see the man. It were that there Podsfoot. I were a bit shocked so I stayed where I was. I dursn't go on that way.' She stopped, pink in the cheeks, gratified to see what effect her words were having.

'Could you hear what they were saying, Miss?' enquired the Inspector.

'Well. I 'eard a bit…. Like I said, 'e was shoutin' at 'er, 'e sounded proper nasty an' angry. I remember, 'e shouted 'I'll give yer one more chance! One more week!''

The Inspector looked at Mabel keenly. 'And you say, you couldn't see who the woman was?'

At this, Mabel looked reluctant. She looked down, then at all the puzzled faces around her. Finally she answered. 'Well, not to be sure, I couldn't. Anyway, she were cryin'. But…..'

'Yes? But what? Please go on, Miss Mabel.'

'Well, she sounded a bit like….. a bit like my mistress, Sir.'

Her words brought forth gasps of shock on all sides, and a few whispers of Rosanna's name. The Inspector persisted. 'Can you just confirm the name of your mistress please?'

'Yes…. I means Mrs. Ponsonby, from The Grange where I works. She's a right lovely lady, ever so pretty an' kind. It upset me to think that Podsfoot man was bein' nasty to 'er. I still gets right upset when I thinks about it. It's dreadful. And now she's so pale an' ill, lyin' on that there posh sofa, weepin', with her bad ankle an' that….'

Mabel was obviously too moved to continue. The Inspector thanked her, then said 'The Reverend told us the lady's suffering from a fall. We'd better talk to Mrs. Ponsonby. As soon as the Constable gets back, I'll send him to fetch her, and her husband. Meanwhile…. Does anyone know anything about the break-in at the antiques shop? Did any of you see or hear anything suspicious? Whoever it was must have worn gloves, there's no finger prints, but someone must know something.'

He gazed expectantly round at the company. Ruby was seen to be whispering with Mabel. Noticing this, he asked 'Miss Ruby, maybe you know something?'

Ruby was very shy and quiet as she mumbled her answer. 'It's just…. it's just….. well, me an' my Fred, we was round in the spinney be'ind the shop yesterd'y, Sund'y. An' we sees Tom Brown.'

'Tom Brown, you say? Who's Tom Brown? And what was he doing?'

Ruby replied 'Well, Tom's jus' a bit of a rascal sometimes. He were there in the trees. Fred an' me, we both saw 'im.'

'What time was this? And what were you and… Fred…. doing there?'

Ruby coloured up at this direct questioning and looked coyly down at her feet in their run-down black work shoes. 'Oh… I s'pose it were around seven o'clock or thereabouts. Me an' my Fred, we was just sort of walkin' along really.'

'I see, seven o'clock. And you were just walking along. Well, that's another two we must talk to…. Tom Brown, and your Fred, whoever he may be.'

The Constable entered noisily, waving a small piece of paper triumphantly. 'Well, Constable, any luck with your enquiries?' asked the Inspector.

'Yes Sir! The Colonel here was right. Mr. Podsfoot..... er, Mr. Talbot, I should say...... was batman in India to a Captain in the army. He was Captain Fitzgibbon....'

'Old Taffy!' cried the Colonel. 'Now I remember!'

'Taffy, Sir?' said the Inspector. 'Was he a Welshman, then?'

'Welsh? No. Not a bit of it. English chappie, but we called him Taffy. It was because of his initials. Theodore Algernon Fitzgibbon, he was. T-A-F. So he was always Taffy to us. Grand chap, athletic. Great at polo, he was!'

At the Colonel's side, his wife appeared to be almost swooning away. She spoke in a dreamy, nostalgic manner. 'Yes! I remember him! So handsome! An Adonis, a real Adonis! And wonderful on the dance floor!'

Taken aback, the Colonel turned to his wife with a censorious expression. 'I didn't know you knew him, Celia! But I do seem to remember he was rather a one for the ladies, come to think of it!'

'Oh yes,' said Celia firmly. 'I knew him, all right! And I wasn't the only one. So romantic....'

The Inspector cut short this exchange with the words 'Please, ladies and gentlemen! I must insist! Carry on, Constable'.

Suspicious glances continued to pass between Celia and her husband. Lady Imogen was observed talking behind her hand to Sir John as Constable Black gave his report.

'Piggy ....er, Major Pratt, I mean..... said this batman, Stanley Talbot, was a no-gooder. Got a dishonourable discharge for dishonesty. Couldn't be trusted, took stuff from the Captain behind his back. Apparently there was quite a to-do. Petty cash, mostly, but some personal things disappeared, papers belonging to the Captain. Mostly letters, Piggy said... I mean, Major Pratt said. Private letters, all vanished. So Mr. Talbot lost his job, and was sent back to Old Blighty.'

The Colonel, the mists of memory now clearing, broke in with confidence. 'That's right, I remember now. It was the talk of the town at the time. Nasty blighter, Talbot. But everyone stuck up for the Captain, old Taffy!'

'Most interesting!' said the Inspector thoughtfully. He turned to the Constable. 'Now, Constable, we have another little job for you. Go into the village, Drift Cottages, and find Tom Brown. Bring him in. Then send for Mrs. Ponsonby. I gather she's hurt her ankle and can't get about too well. In any case, you'd better fetch her husband too.'

'Right you are, Sir!' came from the departing Constable as he bustled out.

'Yes, Inspector, Gerald must come with his wife', said the Reverend. 'I did phone him when we found the body of unfortunate Mr. Podsfoot....'

'Unfortunate, did you say, Bertram?' shrieked Dorothy. 'From what we're hearing, I think he deserved what he got! Not the sort of person we want in our little village at all!'

Her husband turned reproachful eyes on his wife. 'Dorothy, dear, we really must be charitable, we are all but weak mortals....'

'Oh Bertram! Don't be so pious and pompous!' cried his lady wife.

Sir John stepped in to calm troubled waters. 'Dear lady, don't excite yourself! All very upsetting, of course, but as Bertram says, we really must be courteous and let the police do their job, you know!'

Dorothy took a soggy hanky out of her pocket and snuffled into it. 'I'm sorry. I've had rather a trying time these last few days, and really it is all too upsetting. I'm sorry, Bertram dear.'

A knock was heard at the door and in stepped Tom. He stood looking around in surprise at the assembled company. The Inspector addressed him. 'And who are you, young Sir?'

Tom shifted uneasily from foot to foot. 'Me name's Tom Brown. Constable said I were to come 'ere.'

'Ah yes. You were seen in the spinney round behind the antiques shop yesterday evening.... quite late in the evening. Can you tell me what was your purpose in going there please?'

Tom did not want to meet the eye of the Inspector. He was not fond of men in uniform. 'Oh.... nothin' in partic'lar. Jus' enjoyin' a summer evenin', walkin' about the village, you know.'

Ruby spoke. 'You wasn't walkin' much. You was messin' about in the bushes!'

Tom replied huffily. 'I were studyin' nature! Birds an' that! I'm right int'rested in birds!'

This brought a chuckle from Sir John. 'As we in the Magistrates' Court know only too well – very interested in birds, especially game birds!'

Tom scowled and feigned ignorance. The Inspector looked up from his notepad.

'Tom, did you notice anything unusual about Mr. Podsfoot's shop?'

Tom became defensive. ''Ere, don't you try an' pin nuffin on me! We might be poor, us Browns, but that don't make us thieves! I ain't never broke into no shops!'

Ruby spoke up in his defence. 'He weren't near the shop when me an' my Fred saw 'im. He weren't bovvered wiv the shop. But I'd've seen it if them windows was broke. It were just right quiet, not nobody nor nothin' 'appenin' at the shop.'

Tom gave Ruby a grateful nod, then continued studying his boots. The Inspector spoke. 'It seems likely the shop was broken into very late last night, or early this morning. And not by any common thief. Someone was looking for something special.'

As he finished speaking, the door opened to admit the Constable and the Ponsonbys. Rosanna leaned heavily on Gerald's arm. Everyone turned to gaze at them and a stunned silence descended. There was no disguising the miserable state of both Gerald and his wife. Maude looked contrite.

'Oh Rosanna, how are you? I am so sorry about my silly little Dot. It was the thunder, you know. Always sets her off like a mad thing!'

Rosanna's murmured response was barely audible 'I'm much better now, Maude, thank you.'

Lady Imogen touched her arm. 'You don't look too good, Rosanna. We'll have to find you a chair.'

The Colonel jumped up, gallantly offering his chair with the words 'Yes, very pale about the gills. And Gerald, my friend, you must sit here beside your wife.'

The company re-arranged themselves to everyone's satisfaction, and the Inspector resumed his enquiries.

'You are Mrs. Rosanna Ponsonby, I gather? And you are Mr. Gerald Ponsonby, of The Grange?'

Gerald confirmed these facts in the ghost of a voice 'That's right, Sir.'

'And you know we are here to sort out a mystery and a crime? You've heard about the sad accident to Mr. Podsfoot.... or Mr. Talbot, as it now appears?'

Gerald seemed puzzled by the second name. After a moment, he answered wearily 'Yes, I heard Podsfoot was dead.'

At this news Tom, who had been leaning against the wall, leaped forward and gazed around him in terror.

Rosanna emitted a loud shriek 'Dead! Did you say Mr. Podsfoot is dead? Oh, thank the Lord!' She burst into loud tears, covering her face with her hands.

Reverend Valentine looked visibly shocked at this outburst and spoke severely. 'Dear lady, I fear you are not yourself! Gerald, I phoned you as soon as we found the poor man's body. Surely you told the sad news to your wife?'

Gerald, looking exhausted, said levelly 'Bertram, my wife has really not been well these last few days. I had no desire to cause her further grief'. He put his arm protectively around his wife's heaving shoulders.

The Inspector turned to address Tom, who was doing a good impression of a caged lion. 'Do find yourself a chair, Mr. Brown, and keep calm please.'

Tom could not hide his feelings. 'Keep calm?' he shouted. 'Keep calm? You brung me in 'ere, an' I din't know why, an' I ain't done nothin'! And now you talks about a murder! Well it weren't me! I were ovver at Draper's all day, 'oein' turnips in Long Abbeyfield. Jethro Mayes were there wi' me, he can tell you that!'

The Inspector regarded the agitated young man thoughtfully. 'No-one's accusing anyone of anything, Mr. Brown. But it's our job to find out what happened. We must take things one step at a time.' He turned his attention to the Ponsonbys.

'Madam, it seems your husband chose not to tell you the news of Mr. Podsfoot's sad demise. And it seems…. it seems, from your reaction just now, that this is not ….' (he paused to cough apologetically) '….not exactly….. unwelcome news to you.'

Rosanna could not meet his eye. She remained huddled in her chair, her devoted husband regarding her sorrowfully.

The Inspector tried again. 'So, Madam, I'm afraid it's my duty to ask you some painful questions. We have to make a full investigation in cases of this kind. Now, how well did you know Mr. Podsfoot?'

At this Rosanna raised her head to reply with obvious revulsion. 'I…. I didn't know him at all well really. I certainly didn't want to know him.'

'Yet you were seen talking to him, very distressed, not so long ago, I believe?'

Alarm showed in Rosanna's deathly-white face. 'I was seen? When?'

'In the churchyard here, on a Saturday afternoon, about four o'clock. Some angry exchanges took place between you and Mr. Podsfoot.'

Gerald leaped up and stared at his wife in horror. 'Rosanna! Surely there was nothing between you and Mr. Podsfoot? You cannot have cared for that odious man?'

Rosanna was equally horror-stricken. 'Cared for him? I care for Podsfoot? How could you think such a thing, Gerald?'

Gerald sank helplessly back into his chair. As if thinking aloud, he spoke slowly, his voice betraying desolation and despair. 'I don't understand. None of it makes sense. What did he mean, when he said to me "I know more about your wife than you think, much more!" with that horrible leer on his face? Then there were the letters…. In your handwriting! All beginning "Dearest T"! After all, his name was Talbot, that starts with a T, doesn't it?'

Rosanna turned to look at her husband, She looked devastated. 'My letters? What do you know about my letters?' She became engulfed by deep sobs as she spoke. 'I wrote them over twenty years ago…. more than twenty years!

31

And they were all explaining that I loved my husband…. you….. and that what happened on that voyage was a just silly mistake. It meant nothing any more. All that silliness was over! And of course I never sent any letters to Podsfoot, or Mr. Talbot, as he was then. He stole them!'

Everyone appeared to hold their breath. The silent emotional response of the good people of Meadowford suffused the atmosphere. There was excitement, curiosity, sympathy, and shock on every side. The Inspector contemplated Mrs. Ponsonby. She appeared heart-breakingly fragile and vulnerable. He finally broke the silence. 'Mr. and Mrs. Ponsonby, I think you have some explaining to do, both of you. Now, why don't you do the sensible thing, and just tell everything as it happened? That's always best in the end. There's no point in wasting everyone's time, is there?

Gerald was heard to sigh heavily before answering. 'I suppose you're right, Sir. This whole thing is a nightmare, and the sooner it's over, the better.'

Rosanna cast a tender glance towards her suffering husband. 'It will be such a relief to have everything in the open at last. That man has been making my life a misery. But is it true that he's dead? How did that happen?'

'That we don't know, Madam,' replied the Inspector. 'But we will find out. Truth will out, you know!'

Rosanna appeared to have made a decision. She would tell everything. After all, what did she have to lose? 'Well,' she began, 'it was when we were in India. I wasn't happy there. I couldn't stand the heat, and Gerald was so busy. We didn't get much time to ourselves. Oh, there were big parties and receptions and formal dinners. But no real family time. Then the worst thing of all was having to send our little sons to school in England. I missed them so dreadfully, and they missed us, I know.'

Gerald hung his head and made no reply for several minutes. Then he looked at his tearful wife with a hang-dog expression. 'Yes. It's true, I was very occupied with my work. I did realise you were lonely and homesick in India. But it was a good career, I had interesting problems to deal with. I kept hoping things might improve when you got accustomed to the situation, my darling.'

Rosanna's sad memories were now unstoppable. 'I tried, Gerald. I did try to fit in and be a support to you. But whenever I travelled home with Cuthbert and Frederick and left them at school, I felt I had betrayed them. I never could forget their poor dear little faces when I said goodbye. They tried so hard to be brave. But their bottom lips would tremble, and I would see tears in their eyes, every time. It was terrible. I used to call them my brave little soldiers.' She paused to mop her eyes with a sodden hanky. Gerald gave her a gentle hug.

The Inspector could hardly contain his impatience. When would these two middle-aged lovebirds get to the point? He coughed, hoping to prompt more explanations, and Rosanna became aware of his impatience to get on with the case. 'Sorry, Inspector. I'm afraid it is so painful remembering those times. I'll try to go on and tell you what you need to know.'

With an effort, she continued, speaking in a low monotone, not looking at anyone. 'It was ..... it was 1901 when it happened. I boarded the ship to return to India with a heavy heart. I felt miserable and alone, and I couldn't forget those two wistful little faces. And there on the ship ...... it was the 'Victoria Royal'..... I met a handsome young Captain. His name was Theodore. He was so attentive, so kind! I found myself pouring out my unhappiness to him, and he listened. He was so sweet to me. Then he came to my cabin one day.....'

Gerald jumped up angrily, his usually mild blue eyes flashing fire. 'He came to your cabin? The swine!'

The audience was mesmerised. The spell was broken by a murmer from Celia. 'So handsome, such soulful eyes. Just like my spaniel, my little Gingernuts!'

A starchily disapproving comment was heard from Lady Imogen, in a stage whisper to her husband. 'Really, John, sometimes one learns the most surprising things about one's closest friends, doesn't one?'

Sir John motioned her to silence, and the Inspector requested no more interruptions. 'Please continue, Mrs. Ponsonby.'

Rosanna was just audible. 'Well, Theo began to shower me with gifts. Chocolates, flowers, red roses. You could buy them on the ship. I would invite him in and we would talk. We just talked.' Here Rosanna glanced anxiously at the glowering Gerald.

'Then there was a dance one evening, and it was so romantic! We danced..... he moved so beautifully. We walked on deck and gazed at the stars. He knew all the constellations! It was enchanting, so romantic, all my troubles seemed to melt away. Of course, we had champagne and cocktails, and wine with the meals. I suppose one thing led to another. I spent more and more time with him and he was so comforting and gentle....'

A dreadful groan came from Gerald. 'Rosanna, you're breaking my heart!' Remorse and pity showed in Rosanna's features. 'Please don't say that, Gerald! Honestly, as soon as you and I were together again in Madras, I realised it had all been a silly shipboard romance. Really, it meant nothing! I just got foolishly carried away. I knew afterwards that I had been really stupid and disloyal, and the only important things in life were you, and our fine boys, and our life together.' She bestowed on her husband a look of pleading which brought a tear to his eye.

The moment was rudely shattered by a growl from the Colonel. 'That Fitzgibbon was a dashed handsome fellow. Everybody like him, but he could not be trusted with the ladies!' He scowled at Celia. The Inspector frowned at him.

After a moment Gerald's voice was heard. 'And then....' He was obviously struggling to remember those distant times. 'Then, you had a lot to do, around that time. Getting ready for the new baby, our little Flora....'

Gerald was suddenly silent. Those near him saw shock and fear in his face as he stared dumbfounded at his wife. When he eventually spoke, it was with a distinct tremor. 'Our Flora! Such an enchanting little thing, but so unlike our two boys, everyone said so....' Gerald's voice faltered miserably and a stunned silence descended on the crowded room.

Rosanna hastily took up the thread, with a note of desperation. 'Yes, well, of course, she would be different! She's a girl, after all! She definitely takes after my side of the family. I'm told my great grandfather was very dark, really very dark .... with those same lustrous brown eyes!'

Anxiously, Rosanna watched her husband's expression. Her own face was a picture of yearning - for understanding, acceptance, maybe forgiveness. He finally answered.

'Like your great grandfather? Yes, possibly. Yes my darling, I'm sure you're right'. The doubt in his voice belied his words, but he looked bravely into Rosanna's eyes and gave her a smile full of hope and compassion.

The Inspector coughed to break the long silence. No-one else in the room moved a muscle. 'Mrs. Ponsonby, would you care to continue? What was the next turn of events, pray?'

Rosanna turned to face the Inspector and spoke clearly. 'Well, Theodore wrote to me, saying he loved me, and could we meet again. I wrote back, saying I was sorry, but no. It had been a foolish romance. I had just lost my head, but now my feet were back on the ground....'

Maude chuckled. 'That sounds a bit uncomfortable!'

The Inspector sharply asked for no interruptions so Rosanna might continue.

'At first, Theodore wouldn't take no for an answer. He wrote to me again, and I wrote back.' Her voice assumed a nostalgic dreamy tone. 'He even wrote a poem especially for me... a love poem. It went.... let me think .... "How do I love thee? Let me count the ways....."'

A deep laugh erupted from Sir John. 'Are you sure he actually wrote it himself, Rosanna? It sounds deuced familiar, and he didn't write a love poem to me!'

Rosanna was offended. 'That's what he told me,' she said defensively. 'And I was quite moved by it. Anyway, we must have exchanged about half a dozen letters. And at last Theo saw sense, and left me alone.'

Under his breath the Colonel muttered darkly. 'Always the same with these handsome chaps, can't trust them an inch with the ladies!' Everyone ignored him.

Rosanna continued steadily. 'I did my best to make up for my mistake. I wanted to be the best possible wife I could be, for my Gerald. And we were happy, the five of us. I honestly never gave Theo much thought after we returned to England. It was just a foolish episode in the past by then.'

'Thank you for being so frank, Mrs. Ponsonby,' said the Inspector. 'Now could you explain what happened between you and Mr. Podsfoot … I mean, Mr. Talbot?'

Rosanna's face fell. Slowly, she started to relate events, all the company hanging breathless on her every word and looking curiously from her to her husband.

'Well, soon after Podsfoot came to Meadowford Magna and opened the antique shop….. about a year ago…. I started to receive little notes. They were threatening letters really, with no name of the sender. From what was written, I knew whoever it was meant trouble. I was scared to go to the meeting place suggested, our own churchyard. But I was even more scared of what might happen if I did nothing. So I met him. That first time, I had no idea who I was meeting, and I was terrified. It was Podsfoot, of course. I had never known him in India. He told me he had my letters from that time years ago. We always met on a Saturday, four o'clock, in the churchyard, under the yew trees. It was a hideous situation. It made me feel quite ill.'

The Inspector asked 'I suppose he asked for money?'

'Yes,' said Rosanna bleakly. 'Lots of money. More than I could afford. Five guineas a week, he wanted, or he would show the letters to Gerald.' Her voice shook and she stopped to blow her nose and regain her composure.

'He told me he had all my letters to Theodore. I had destroyed the ones Theo sent to me, years ago. I even destroyed his lovely poem.'

Sir John was heard to give a snort of laughter at this remark. Lady Imogen frowned at him.

Disconcerted, Rosanna paused for a few moments, then went bravely on.

'I didn't want to read those letters again anyway, they only made me feel upset and guilty. After all, it was only a silly moment in the past.'

She glanced anxiously at Gerald, who had been gazing at her sorrowfully as she told her story. He now put a protective arm around her and held her close.

'My poor Rosanna! Why didn't you tell me? I know I neglected you shamefully sometimes, in those days. I had a huge work load and I often needed to go away. But it all happened so long ago now - ancient history! I would have forgiven you. I could have gone round and punched Podsfoot on the nose!'

'Mr. Ponsonby, are you a violent man?' asked the Inspector ominously.

'No, no, Officer! It was just a figure of speech!' protested Gerald. 'What I really would have done, is report the whole matter to you, to the police.'

'And that's just what your wife should have done. We would have helped her. Blackmail is a nasty crime. We've no sympathy for blackmailers.'

Murmurs of assent were heard all round – 'Wicked!' 'Cruel and nasty!' 'Beastly man!'

Rosanna seemed to sit up straighter. Her voice sounded stronger and more confident as she continued. 'Yes, it was very, very nasty and I was at my wits' end. At first, I gave him my savings, and the money my mother left me. Then I started to give him jewellery. It was a dreadful wrench, giving that vile man the lovely things that I had been given over the years. Some from my parents, and some from you of course, darling.'

She turned sorrowful eyes on her husband, who patted her shoulder gently. With an effort she continued, her voice shaky and low. 'But that wasn't always enough to keep the brute quiet. You see, some of my favourite necklaces and brooches, which I had always believed were valuable, turned out to be only imitation. That maddened Podsfoot. Soon I had nothing much left to give, and Podsfoot became more and more aggressive and angry. I was terrified of him. At the garden party on Saturday, he passed me a note. I've lost it somehow, but I remember exactly what he had written. It went -

"I am not a patient man. You owe me fifty guineas. Meet me, same time, same place. No paste this time or your husband will know all and your marriage will be over." '

Gerald leaped from his chair, shouting. 'So THAT'S what it meant! No more paste – no more imitation jewellery! I was mystified by the reference to paste! All I could think of was meat paste…. or fish paste … sandwiches!'

Rosanna stared wide-eyed at her apparently deranged husband. 'Gerald! Did you find that note? It was in my jacket pocket and I lost my jacket somehow. Left it in Celia's garden I suppose. Well…. I was terrified because I no longer had anything to give that beastly man, no money, nothing of value at all. But I resolved to meet Podsfoot and plead with him, as soon as the garden party was over. I would beg him to keep my secret and not tell you. But I sprained my ankle. I couldn't walk a step. There was no way I could meet him and I was just terrified! I've just been lying at home, going out of my mind, since Saturday!

'Poor you, Rosanna!' interjected Maude. 'I'll give my Dotty what for when she finally comes home, the baggage!'

The Inspector thanked Rosanna for her frankness, and turned to Gerald. 'Now it's your turn, Mr. Ponsonby, Sir. What have you got to say?'

Gerald's face wore a look of resignation and relief. He swallowed, then began to speak steadily. 'I suppose I should tell you everything, Officer. I don't want anyone else blamed for what happened. But of course it was just an accident.'

'That's right, Sir, just tell me in your own words,' encouraged the Inspector.

'It was on Saturday, after the garden party. I had a little job to do for the Vicar. He asked me to carry a large gift for his wife, and hide it in his garden shed.'

Dorothy's worn face lit up as she turned towards her husband. 'Bertram! A large gift, for me? How delightful!'

Reverend Valentine smiled lovingly at his long-suffering wife. 'Yes, my dear! I chose it carefully, most carefully, and I'm sure you'll love it!'

Gerald interrupted these fond exchanges, speaking ruefully. 'I'm afraid you won't be able to love it, Dorothy, because I had to burn it!'

Dorothy was appalled. 'You had to burn my gift, Gerald? Whatever can you mean?'

'Now, now, ladies and gentlemen,' said the Inspector, 'Please do allow Mr. Ponsonby to continue.'

Dorothy subsided, disappointment etched on her face. She and Bertram exchanged bewildered glances as the story unfolded.

'Well, by chance, as I left The Gables when the garden party was rained off, I saw my wife's blue linen jacket lying on a chair. I picked it up to take it home for her. I assumed she was in Celia's kitchen with the other ladies, washing up the tea things. I decided to go to the Vicarage garden via the churchyard. That way, I was less likely to meet Dorothy and give the game away.' Gerald paused, passing his hand wearily across his eyes, before continuing. 'Well, I was plodding around the tombstones, my head down because the rain was falling in torrents. I suddenly came upon Podsfoot, under the yew trees. He was sitting on a tombstone, like some grotesque goblin! I nearly fell over him.'

'At what time did this meeting occur please, Mr. Ponsonby?' enquired the Inspector.

'Oh, I suppose soon after four o'clock, Sir. Well, Podsfoot looked up at me and said "Where is your pretty wife, Mr. Ponsonby? Has she sent you to talk to me?"

I hated hearing him talk about my wife in that familiar way. He had a horrible sneer on his ugly face. He was very sure of himself. I don't remember exactly what I said to him. It was something like "I'd rather you didn't speak of my wife in that tone, Sir!" Because I never liked the fellow. He was sort of unclean, somehow.'

At this point various murmured comments were exchanged around the room. The Inspector heard 'Filthy brute!' 'Monster!' and other uncharitable remarks. After a brief pause, Gerald continued.

'Well, he answered me with a horrible laugh! He said "Quite a looker, your wife, isn't she?" I saw red. I never meant to touch him, honestly. But I suppose I sort of lunged towards him. Trouble was, I had the Vicar's gift over my shoulder. It was in a sack, and it was very heavy. When I leaned towards Podsfoot, it swung forward and got him right on the forehead with such a thump! He fell, backwards, hitting his head on a jagged broken tombstone. I never saw so much blood! I'd dropped the sack, and Rosanna's jacket – it was slippery underfoot because of the rain. I sort of skidded towards Podsfoot and I put out my hands to stop myself falling.

Somehow, the sack and the jacket were both on the ground where he lay. The blood just gushed from the wounds on his skull...'

Gerald stopped, overcome by the horror of remembering. Gasps came from those around him but no-one spoke. Gerald recovered himself and went on.

'I panicked. But it was not likely anyone would come, in the pouring rain, and I hoped Podsfoot was just stunned. I picked up Rosanna's jacket, which was badly bloodstained, and gave it a little shake. Out of the pocket dropped a folded piece of paper. When I read it, I just froze. My blood ran cold, you could say. What could it mean? "Your marriage will be over!" and "I will tell your husband all!"

I realised Podsfoot had some sort of hold over Rosanna. So I decided I should go to his shop before going to get help, and find out what it was all about. Anyway, because of the blood, I couldn't take the elephant's foot to the Vicar's garden shed...'

Here Gerald was interrupted by a horrified squeal from Dorothy. 'Elephant's foot? Did you say elephant's foot, Gerald?'

'Yes, that's what your present was to be, Dorothy!' replied Gerald lamely.

Dorothy turned an enraged face towards her surprised husband. 'Bertram! What would I want with an elephant's foot? For goodness sake!'

'But.... But my dear,' stammered the shrinking Bertram, 'It was a remarkable object! Carefully crafted into a most impressive umbrella stand! Just the ticket!'

'Please, please!' came the Inspector's voice. 'Allow Mr. Ponsonby to continue.'

'I knew I had to hide the wretched elephant's foot. I dragged it over the low wall into the field, and hid it under that old scarecrow's long black coat. It's a long draggly coat, hangs right down to the soil.'

Maude chipped in. 'So that's what attracted my Dotty! I expect she smelt the blood on the sack. I just couldn't get her to come away!'

Once again, the Inspector appealed for silence. Gerald continued to relate his story, gazing blindly downwards, not meeting anyone's eye.

'I needed time to search the shop and find out what was going on. I went home to wash the blood off Rosanna's jacket and my blazer, while I decided what to do next. I went into the outhouse and filled a bucket from the outside tap. I rubbed and scrubbed those blessed clothes but the bloodstains still showed.

As evening fell, I began to panic. I couldn't leave Podsfoot in the churchyard. The next day was Sunday, there would be people everywhere. Then Monday – that's when Charlie Brown always cuts the grass.'

Tom, with suspicion now falling on others, felt much more at ease. He was even beginning to enjoy the excitement. He called out brightly. 'Yeah, that's me Dad's job, fer the Vicar. He does the churchyard, and 'is garden, on a Monday'. The Inspector put his finger to his lips and Tom obediently fell silent.

'Podsfoot had to disappear,' said Gerald wearily. 'But where to? I was desperate. I looked around. Beyond the shrubbery in the Vicarage garden, I could just see the open coal chute in the back yard. That's when the idea came to me. Sorry, Bertram, it was wrong of me. But I just didn't know what to do.'

The Reverend said mildly 'Not a very neighbourly act, Gerald, dumping a corpse on me!'

'I am so sorry, Bertram. I really can't tell you how sorry I am. It won't happen again!' Gerald was contrite. 'At that stage, I still thought the pouring rain might wake the man up. Maybe he was just unconscious. But I dare not do more until it was dark.' Once again, Gerald paused to collect his thoughts.

'So...... I crept home, wet through and with mud all over my shoes. That's when I found out about Rosanna's accident. I didn't know what to say to her. My head was in a whirl, with that man's words spinning around – "Quite a looker, your wife, isn't she!" I was struggling to understand what it could mean. And Rosanna seemed terribly upset. After an hour or two I made her a warm drink and tucked a thick blanket around her, and she started to doze. It was nearly midnight by then. I put on an old gardening coat and crept out, back to the churchyard. Thank goodness the rain had stopped. The blood on Podsfoot's head was dry and crusty and he hadn't moved. So I knew beyond doubt that he was stone dead.

I heaved the body over my shoulder. It wasn't so much heavier than that darned elephant's foot really. I dragged it over the wall and into the back courtyard. Then I just shoved him into the Vicar's open coal chute. I know it was stupid. But I was so shocked, I wasn't thinking straight. I went home to bed, but I never slept a wink.'

Rosanna had been hanging on Gerald's every word, her face a mask of horror. Now she cried out pitifully through her tears. 'Oh Gerald darling! What a mess I've got us both into! I am so sorry.'

Gerald looked at her with gratitude and love. 'I hope you can forgive me, Rosanna. It was an accident, but that man made me see red! I got up at first light and got the blazer and jacket from the outhouse. Then I hurried to the beanfield where the bloody sack was hidden. Excuse my French, but it really was a bloody sack, and the blood had soaked into the elephant hide. It was a disgusting mess. I put the clothes inside the sack and hid the lot in the hedge.

I went into the churchyard to check the place where the accident happened. Luckily, the rain had washed away most of the bloodstains on the stones and grass there. I tipped a few more bucketfuls over the place, just to make sure. Then, I had a go at washing that damned elephant's foot. I took buckets of soapy water out....'

 Maude cried out 'So that's why you were carrying a bucket of suds around! Thought it was rum at the time!'

'That's right,' resumed Gerald. 'I started to see people here and there, dog-walkers and so on, like you, Maude. So I had to find somewhere off the beaten track. I knew people would soon be coming to the church. So I dragged the sack into the spinney behind the shops. It's very overgrown there, all brambles and nettles between the trees and bushes. I had another go at cleaning the elephant's foot, but it was hopeless. So I went home to find paper and kindling, and paraffin to make sure, and then I started a fire. It took hours to burn everything. I used a lot of paraffin, and I hunted around for dry stuff under the fallen leaves, to keep the thing going. Luckily I found a few thick fallen branches. At last there was nothing left except ashes, a few buttons, and the heavy disk of metal from the base of the elephant's foot. Then I slunk back home.'

Tom could not restrain himself. He grinned and said with admiration 'That were some fire you made, Mr. Ponsonby! Them ashes stayed red fer ages!'

Gerald looked up. 'Sorry, Bertram! Sorry, Dorothy!' He then sat looking the picture of woe, his head in his hands. Murmurs of sympathy filled the room.

The Inspector spoke calmly. 'Thank you, Mr. Ponsonby. You have been very helpful. But now I need you to tell me about the break-in at the shop, please.'

With an effort, Gerald sat up and raised his head. Rosanna pulled her chair nearer to his and laid her hand on his knee. Everyone listened intently.

'Oh yes, the shop. Well, that was early Monday morning, about four in the morning I think. I haven't had a good night's sleep since last Friday. Of course, I knew the shop was empty. I broke the back window to get in.... cut my arm as well. I searched his office, wrenching open drawers and up-ending boxes. I found loads of papers and hundreds of pounds in notes. There were bundles of letters tied up with string. I opened them all. I recognised Rosanna's handwriting … it was just one of the smaller bundles of letters, and the ink was quite faded. They were addressed to "Dearest T", which made me wonder whether the T was for Talbot … whether there could have been some relationship between Rosanna and that swine Podsfoot!'

Rosanna could not bear this. 'Dearest, how could you think such a thing?'

Gerald tenderly took his wife's hand and looked into her eyes. 'Well …. I was confused, shocked, terrified and exhausted all at once. I didn't know what to think. I suppose I'll end up in jail now. What a mess!'

The Inspector spoke kindly. 'You appear to have held nothing back, Mr. Ponsonby. We'll have to go through your account carefully at the police station, and check all the details, of course. But if you get a really good solicitor to make a case for you....'

Sir John interrupted heartily, coming to stand by Gerald. 'I know just the fellow, Gerald. Best Counsel in the land. He'd have got Jack the Ripper off the hook!'

'Thank you, John, but please don't compare me to Jack the Ripper! It was an accident, after all!' exclaimed Gerald.

The Inspector now spoke severely. 'An accident maybe, Sir. But you took great care to hide a mountain of evidence and pervert the course of justice, you know.'

'I can't deny it,' said Gerald wearily. 'I know I've done a lot of very stupid things.'

The Colonel joined Sir John, putting a friendly hand on Gerald's shoulder. 'It could happen to anyone, Gerald! When a chap sees red like that, common sense goes out of the window. We will all vouch for your good character, old chum.'

The residents of Meadowford Magna now watched entranced as Rosanna slid to her knees before her husband, grasping his hands and looking into his ravaged visage with adoration. 'I'll wait for you, my dearest darling, if you go to prison.... However long it takes!'

Overcome, Gerald could only nod dumbly. The Inspector broke the spell.

'Miss Ruby, we have all the evidence we need, so I won't after all be needing to talk to your friend Fred. Thank you all for your help, and thank you, Vicar, and your lady wife, for your hospitality.'

He turned his attention to the Ponsonbys. 'Mr. and Mrs. Ponsonby, I must ask you both to accompany me to Upper Abbeyfield Police Station, please. Everyone else is free to leave.'

At these words, Constable Black leaped eagerly forward, producing handcuffs from his deep pockets.

'Er, thank you, Constable,' said the Inspector, 'but I don't think we will require those things today.'

Reverend Valentine turned solicitously towards his wife. 'Dorothy dear, I am so sorry about your present. Maybe you'd like some flowers, chocolates, silk stockings, perfume.... that sort of thing, instead?'

A shudder of revulsion shook Dorothy as she replied with feeling. 'Of course, Bertram dear. I'm glad that nasty old relic is gone.'

The Colonel joined in. 'Nasty old relic, did you say, Dorothy? Do you mean that Podsfoot cove?'

'Of course not, Mortimer!' answered Dorothy. 'We shouldn't speak ill of the dead, you know! I mean, the stuffed elephant's foot umbrella stand!'

THE END

MISCHIEF IN MEADOWFORD

ONE – A WALK IN THE WOODS

Maude's brogues were heavy with mud as she emerged into the clearing that served as garden to 'Lone Cottage'. Dusk was falling, accompanied by a searching Autumn mist. The complaints of her niece, Celia, who was a few yards in her wake, assaulted Maude's ears. Trailing brambles caught Celia's jacket and low branches scraped her face; she was fed up with her Aunt's demands. Behind the two women, Celia's husband Mortimer crashed through the bushes like a wounded buffalo.

Reaching the clearing, the three stood regarding the ruinous cottage. It was almost beyond belief that two elderly women called this isolated, ramshackle place home.

'Dotty! Dotty!' screeched Maude into the gloom. There was no answering bark. The Colonel felt he was getting beyond this kind of lark. His breath came in gasps and he thought wistfully of his own fireside and his beloved pipe. Maude and her ridiculous little dog Dotty took up far more time than he would have chosen. But really, what choice did he have? The old girl was in her seventies now.

'Maude, do you think Dotty may just have run home?' he asked wearily.

'That dog's a darned nuisance, Aunt!' snapped Celia. Why she can't come when she's called, like my Gingernuts always does, I do not know!'

For answer, Maude called again. 'Dotty! Where is that dratted dog?'

'Ssh, Maude,' said Mortimer, 'You'll scare those old Pentelow sisters to death, screeching outside their cottage in the dark.'

'But are they at home?' mused Celia. 'There's no light showing anywhere. Look, the curtains aren't closed and the door's wide open!'

'Rum old girls, those two,' remarked Maude. 'Both half dippy if you ask me. Pushing eighty now and they always were a bit weird.'

'Aunt, do be quiet!' said Celia crossly. 'They'll hear you. They must be in there, where else would they be at half past seven in the evening?'

The Colonel sounded thoughtful. 'Must be hard for 'em out here with no neighbours. Better make sure they're OK I suppose.'

'Give them a knock, then, Mortimer – see what's going on,' suggested Celia.

Maude was restless. 'I can't hang about, got to find that dratted hound of mine. Maybe I'll go home - Dotty might have turned up by now. Cheerio.'

Maude's stocky form disappeared through the trees. Her stentorian calls to her dog gradually faded away.

Mortimer knocked on the worn plank door. Silence. An owl hooted, apparently only yards away. Celia jumped, shivered violently, and grabbed her husband's sleeve.

'Try again, Mortimer! They're both deaf as posts, I believe!'
A second knock had no effect and the two stood uncertain, waiting and listening.

'Do you think we should go in, Mortimer?' asked Celia doubtfully.

'Why not? After all, we're not being nosey, just neighbourly,' came the gruff reply. 'We'd better check they're all right. Funny the door's open.'
Celia put her head through the low doorway. 'Hello! Elfrida! Gladys! May we come in?' No answer.

Celia ventured a few steps into the shadowy interior of the one-up, one-down cottage, dragging her husband behind her. He coughed loudly to announce their presence. The silhouettes of the two elderly sisters, sitting either end of a table, were just visible in the twilight. An oil lamp in the centre of the table seemed to have burned out. The odour of cheap paraffin lingered in the air.

'Good evening, ladies, forgive the intrusion. You know us – Colonel Blunkett and the wife. We were just passing and we noticed your door was open .....'
A sudden scuffling and clucking caused Celia to grab nervously at her husband's arm, as two bedraggled hens scuttled out from under the table and made their escape through the open doorway, disappearing into the twilight.

Tentatively, the Colonel touched the shoulder of the nearest sister, who was slouched awkwardly in an ancient chair of rough-hewn wood. Her head in its raggedy cloth bonnet was tipped strangely sideways against the high-backed chair.

As he withdrew his hand, to his horror the wizened little body slithered sideways, then slid down onto the brick floor.

Celia leaped back towards the door emitting a piercing scream. 'Mortimer! You clumsy brute! You've knocked her off her chair!'

'Jeepers! Well blow me down!' exclaimed her husband, staring in bewilderment at the huddled bundle of clothes at his feet. He nudged the body with his foot, recoiling as he felt the total lack of response.

'Nonsense, Celia, I only just touched her, light as a feather, and down she went! Come on, you were in the Red Cross, check her over! Let's see what's up with the other old girl.'

Gingerly, he stepped through the gloom to peer into the face of the other sister, which was difficult as her head and shoulders were slumped on the table.

'Hello m'dear.... Gladys, isn't it? Bit pale about the gills, eh? Off colour today?'

Celia gently rolled old Elfrida's body over on the cold brick floor. She did

44

not like what she saw. Celia seemed to have lost the power of speech and could only swallow nervously as she moved to join her husband, full of apprehension. Summoning her failing courage, she lifted the strands of unkempt dry hair that hid the face of the second sister, whose shoulders were slumped on the table. She prodded the unyielding grey flesh. There was just enough light to distinguish a pair of blank staring eyes and a gaping toothless mouth. Celia stood as if frozen beside her horrified husband, finally articulating what they were both thinking, her usually strident voice emerging as the merest bat-squeak.

'Not off colour, Mortimer, but dead! They're both stone dead! Poor old things!' She glanced around the cluttered room. A blackened pot stood on a trivet beside the mean little grate, which held only cold ashes. The unappetising remains of a meal were in bowls on the table, with a crust or two, and mugs in which tea leaves reposed. One mug lay sideways in a small pool of tea. A strange stale smell hung in the air, mingling with the odour of various bunches of drying herbs, tied round with string, which dangled from the beams above.

As the Colonel moved around the low room – little more than a hovel – the herbs brushed against his face and head, increasing his feelings of panic as he tried to make sense of the scene. What a pitiful end to the unremarkable, joyless lives of two helpless old women. He turned to his wife, his face full of helpless pity. 'What a way to die. Of course, you're right, old gal, they've both snuffed it! Bit of a coincidence, both dying together, though, in the middle of a meal.... smells a bit like fish, I'd say. They don't seem to be injured at all. Wonder what happened?'

Celia had pulled herself together and was regaining her usual business-like command of every situation. 'Goodness knows! Whatever happened here is a mystery for a doctor to solve, and for the police. So come on, Mortimer, it's back home for us to phone for help.' She marched purposefully towards the open door.

'Hoi, wait for me, old gel! The legs are a bit wobbly, we should stick together,' said Mortimer, stumbling after his wife. It was his turn to grab her by the arm now. Glad to leave the desolate scene, they quickened their steps, the Colonel using his trusty Malacca cane to swipe at trailing brambles encroaching on the narrow pathway. Full of trepidation they hurried home through the gathering darkness to raise the alarm.

TWO – RUMOURS AND THEORIES

By the following day the news had spread throughout Meadowford, and little clusters of villagers could be seen, excited heads close together as they elaborated the known facts. Maude, who in fact had not even entered the cottage, was bubbling over with importance as she and her niece Celia held court in Low Lane. The little group included Phoebe, wife of Doctor Jones, and Sir John and Lady Imogen Greenleaf of Old Hall.

Maude was keeping everyone up to date with developments. 'So then, when I found her, she was nosing around a dead cat. Scraggy old thing, a ginger Tom. Stretched out on the grass, dead as a doornail! Of course my Dotty couldn't get enough of the smell. She was wriggling and snuffling around…..'

Sir John interrupted urgently. 'But the two old women! Phoebe, what happened to them? We heard Walter was called to the cottage late yesterday evening….'

Phoebe, very correct in her green knitted two-piece and neat little hat, was glad to oblige, in conspiratorial mode. 'Well, Walter and I were just sitting down to listen to the wireless, after supper, when Constable Black knocked on our door. He took Walter away with him. Just said a doctor was needed….'

Phoebe was interrupted by Maude, keen to finish her tale. '….so there was nothing to do but get her in the bath there and then! Couldn't have that smell in the house!'

Lady Imogen gave a horrified squeak. 'Get her in the bath, did you say, Maude! Surely not! How perfectly gruesome!'

'Bath my Dotty, I mean, not those poor old hags, Imogen!' explained Maude. 'Had to get rid of the dead cat pong, y'know!'

Celia said thoughtfully 'Talking of smells, it was a bit whiffy in the cottage. Smelt a bit like rotting fish, I thought.'

Sir John was becoming impatient. 'But what did Walter say, Phoebe? Could he say how Elfrida and Gladys died?'

'Well, really he was hardly allowed to touch them. Seems it might be a crime scene. He only had to confirm that the poor old things were dead. Then I gather the police pathologist and photographers were set to work,' replied Phoebe.

Maude could not contain herself. 'Yes, that's right. This morning I just thought I'd walk my Dotty over to Lone Cottage. Not that I was being a nosey parker or anything. Wouldn't dream of it. But my Dotty loves that bit of woodland, so wild, lovely holes to scrabble in….'

'And dead cats for extra excitement, I suppose!' chipped in Celia with rather an edge to her voice. Maude was not abashed.

'Yes…. funny you should say that. Seems the police took away the old moggy for examination as well! Might provide evidence, they said. I just happened to overhear them discussing things as I passed, you know.'

Celia gave her elderly Aunt a look of exasperation.

Lady Imogen was next to speak. 'Those two old girls used to come charring for us years ago. It's a bit embarrassing that the cottage is on our estate. It's seen better days, we know.' A defensive note crept into her voice. 'But the old girls wanted to stay there, it was their home. So we let them have it for a few pence a week.'

'They were sisters, of course,' put in Sir John. 'Born in the village, been here all their lives. Never married. Eccentric, but quite harmless.'

Reminiscences and opinions now flooded in from all sides.

'…bound to be talk, with them dying together like that. Can't have been a robbery. Why would anyone bother?'

'….yes, nothing but rubbishy sticks of furniture in there. No tablecloth even, Mortimer said. They lived on poor relief.'

'….and our dear Vicar always made sure they got the odd food parcel, a few warm clothes after jumble sales…'

'….and they had that scrappy little vegetable plot. I've seen Charlie Brown doing a bit of work in that garden. Good-hearted family, those Browns…'

'I've heard there will be an inquest next week,' remarked Sir John.

Lady Imogen looked anxiously at her husband. 'Unexplained deaths and inquests! On our own estate, too! I'm afraid tongues will wag, you know what gossips the village people are! It's really too bad!'

Sir John was calm and reassuring. 'Yes, yes, But don't upset yourself, my dear. Come on home now. I'd like a bit of peace before we go over to the Vicarage to discuss the funeral service.'

'No relatives at all, to help!' said Maude. 'Funny life, getting old in that ruin of a place, with spooky woods all round and no young 'uns to help them out. No wonder they went a bit batty!'

Lady Imogen feared that her husband's generosity as landlord was being called into question. She sniffed into a tiny white hanky before replying coldly. 'One does one's best to help, do the right thing….. it all costs time and money, you know!'

Her husband gently took her arm. 'Don't upset yourself, Imo my dear. Come on home now'. He guided her firmly back towards the Old Hall, first courteously bidding farewell to the assembled company.

Celia turned to Phoebe and Maude, her face animated. 'It's not all death and disaster, you know. Don't forget we're all invited to cocktails at Wood Hall next week.'

Maude was all enthusiasm. 'Yes, next Saturday! High time we had a party! Haven't been inside Wood Hall for donkey's years! All our crowd will be there. Can't wait to see inside the old place again.'

'What a shame Gerald and Rosanna won't be able to come along,' said Celia. 'They both love a party.'

'Yes,' said Phoebe wistfully. 'I do miss Rosanna, she's been away such a lot since poor Gerald.... er..... had to leave us.'

Maude was working out dates. 'Yes, I believe the sentence was seven years, commuted to four for good behaviour, and Gerald is normally well-behaved!' She gave a deep chuckle. 'And....if memory serves me right it's now more than three years since – as you so tactfully put it, Phoebe – he had to leave us!'

Celia said 'I believe Rosanna's up in Scotland at the moment, staying with Flora and her family. Rosanna went around telling everyone she was off for a golfing holiday this time. But it's a pity she won't be back before Saturday's fun and games.'

'Yes, it's bad luck,' said Phoebe. You're right, Celia, she always loved parties and we don't often have them in Meadowford. This cocktail party should be interesting. Seems it's old Hepzibah's ninetieth birthday, Haven't set eyes on her for ages. That's something to look forward to, take our minds off this gruesome Pentelow business. Well, I must be off now, nice to see you all.'

The friends went their separate ways, enlivened by the thought of next week's jollities, and vowing to keep each other updated on any news they might hear about the unexplained deaths at Lone Cottage.

A few days later, Rev. Bertram Valentine and his lady wife were strolling along the lane when they came upon Celia and Phoebe, deep in conversation.

'Why, just the ladies I hoped to see!' cried Bertram, smiling hopefully at his two parishioners. 'I have a favour to ask of you dear ladies, if you please!'

'Have you, Bertram?' said Celia. 'Fire away then!'

'It's about the funeral, you see,' began Bertram. 'There's no relatives to help. Do you think you might be so kind as to find some flowers – maybe some foliage too – for the church, for our poor departed, on Thursday? Church looks so bare without flowers and after all, those two sisters lived their whole lives in our village. Sir John is most graciously paying for the funeral, since they were his tenants.'

Here his wife Dorothy interrupted him to murmur 'So kind, such a gentleman! But we do feel we can't impose further on him and his good lady. So we wondered if you might feel inclined....'

'...... flowers provide that little extra touch, show that we do care, if you know what I mean.' continued her husband in his best persuasive tones.

'Yes of course, Vicar,' said Phoebe, 'and we'll come to the service, won't we, Celia? So sad not to have a good send off, I always think.'

'They were a crummy old pair,' said Celia in her usual blunt manner. 'I suppose they did their best. They were quite well known for their home-brewed health cures. That's a joke, in the circumstances!'

'Yes,' pondered Dorothy, 'I hear they were quite in demand for herbal cures in the past. So it's particularly ironic that they should have inadvertently poisoned themselves.'

'That's the story, yes,' said Celia, 'poisonous mushrooms – nasty!'

'What ho! Talking about poisonous mushrooms, look who's coming!' said Rev. Bertram, gazing down the lane. Everyone turned to look. A curiously attired couple were slowly approaching. The man, pipe in mouth as always, was stocky, with grey beard and moustache. He wore an ancient leather jacket, thick trousers tucked into leather boots, and a battered leather hat with bright pheasant feathers tucked into the brim. A red neckerchief knotted around his throat lent a rakish air to his appearance.

The woman wore a dirndl skirt with braid trim, a man's raincoat, thick wrinkled wool stockings and gumboots. She had a floral neckerchief over her grey hair, knotted under her chin. Over her arm was a round basket which the two were busily filling with blackberries from the hedgerows.

'Oh yes, it's Svetla and Ivan!' said Celia. 'Maude told me they were called in to help the police identify those dreadful mushrooms!'

'Perhaps they'll explain things to us,' said Phoebe. 'After all, we need to know these dangers. Can't be too careful, as Walter always says.'

The newcomers stopped their blackberry-gathering as they realised the group of villagers were all looking hopefully towards them, their faces eager. The couple were becoming accustomed to being accosted wherever they went by curious villagers wanting to know all the details leading to the demise of the Pentelow sisters.

Reverend Valentine spoke for the little group of friends as soon as Svetla and Ivan were in earshot. 'Good morning, dear friends. I hear you've been able to help the police with their enquiries into last week's tragic event. Interesting, most interesting!'

Svetla answered in her rather quaintly accented English. 'Good morning, Vicar …. and everybody. Yes, that's right, we told nice Inspector everything we know.'

Ivan stepped up smartly, almost appearing to stand to attention before the Reverend. Ivan doffed his hat with a slight formal bow. 'Fine day, isn't it, Sir, and ladies'. He looked around the group. All eyes were fixed on him, gleaming with curiosity. 'Fine weather for fungus foray, I'd say …. if you know what you're doing, that is.'

Like his wife, Ivan had mastered the English language almost perfectly during the three and a half decades since they had left their native Bohemia. Having spent hours discussing horses with Miss Hepzibah and the racing elite, their grammar was perfect, except for one curious trait. This was, that neither of them had ever seen the need to acquire the English habit of preceding all nouns with definite or indefinite articles – 'the' or 'a'. This omission gave to most of their utterances a distinctly 'foreign' ring.

The Vicar went straight to the point. 'I understand your expert knowledge has cleared up some mysteries. An unfortunate mistake, it seems?'

Svetla answered. 'That's right, Reverend. You see, in Old Bohemia, everyone picks all kinds of mushrooms. Right from being little children, we were taught how to tell one kind from another.'

'There's hundreds of different varieties,' said Ivan. 'Most of them are delicious. Only few are poisonous. Poor old women made elementary mistake in identification.'

Dorothy sighed. 'Most unfortunate, most sad! I suppose they had impaired eyesight, being so elderly.'

Heads were nodded around the group. Everyone tried to assume expressions of deep sorrow and sympathy.

Celia was first to resume. 'Funny. Because I know they picked plenty of mushrooms in their time. I remember seeing them on my early morning jaunts, up with the lark. Bent double in the meadows and woods, picking like crazy. They'd have whole baskets full...... not just the ordinary ones you get in shops. All shapes and sizes.'

Ivan nodded in agreement. 'Yes. But you do need good eyesight and good nose. Unless you're expert you need good illustrated reference book to be safe.'

'It seems they made mushroom sauce to go with some fish they had for supper,' said Svetla. 'Mushrooms they found just by Great Wood, I think. Fly Agaric in your books.'

Ivan joined in. 'Yes, Fly Agaric. It's one of Amanitas, related to Death Cap and Destroying Angel.'

Celia was bemused. 'Fly Agaric? What a peculiar name. Weird!'

'Yes. Fly Agaric,' repeated Ivan. 'That's because back in medieval times, people used it to kill flies. They'd mix bits of it with milk. Flies would come, suck up liquid, and fall into coma. Just like that!' He demonstrated with his work-worn hands - a swerving swarm of flies, zooming down to suck (he made a slurping noise), then splat! Down they crashed as if dead.

Svetla picked up the tale. 'But flies don't die from mushroom. People would squash them while they lay still. That way they kept house free of dirty flies.'

Dorothy looked thoughtful. 'Did you say this poisonous Agaric fungus has a red cap?' She shuddered. 'I wouldn't dare eat a mushroom which was red. Red's usually a warning colour, isn't it?'

'Maybe,' said Svetla. 'But there's plenty of tasty mushrooms with red caps.'

'Yes,' agreed Ivan. 'Scarlet Hood, Orange Birch Boletus, Meadow Wax Cap, some Russulas. All quite delicious.'

'Good Lord!' exclaimed Rev. Valentine, hastily adding 'I mean, goodness gracious! I didn't know that!'

Ivan was warming to his theme. 'Yes, but you see good mushroom gatherers know that Fly Agaric has white bumps all over cap, that's important point of identification. Means danger!'

'You see,' said Svetla, we had lot of rain last week. Heavy rain washes away white bumps. Then it's more confusing.'

Rev. Valentine looked around at his friends and neighbours. He then spoke with relief in his voice. 'Well, friends, it's a blessing to us all that you, dear Ivan and Svetla, were able to help. It was a most unwelcome possibility when we wondered – just wondered – whether our old folk were safe from attack in their own homes!'

All around the little circle heads were nodded and meaningful looks exchanged.

Dorothy turned to Svetla to ask a question. 'Would the Pentelows have suffered much before they died, do you think, Svetla?'

Svetla reassured her with the words 'No, it's not as horrible as Death Cap poisoning. First symptom is twitching. Queer uncontrolled twitching, soon after eating.'

'Then you go dizzy,' added Ivan, 'then you fall into deep sleep. Almost unconsciousness.'

'Those poor old women were half-starved and weak. So they probably died during deep sleep stage,' said Svetla.

Ivan became more animated, leaning forward and tapping the side of his nose with a forefinger for emphasis. 'They say Fly Agaric is used in Lapland at parties. Rather like alcohol over here. Because after deep sleep stage, you wake up seeing wonderful visions. Hallucinating. Your nerves are on high alert.'

Svetla said 'Sometimes people end up hopping and skipping about, in kind of dance of madness!'

Celia gave a snort of laughter. 'Those poor old gals didn't do much dancing though!'

'You see,' went on Svetla, 'it's not fatal to strong, healthy people who only eat little bit.'

Rev. Valentine's face was full of concern. 'But those poor dear Pentelow sisters were not young and strong. So sad, so sad!'

Murmurs of agreement arose on all sides. Celia broke the subdued silence.

'How peculiar. So glad we met you. Mortimer will be fascinated. Poor old chap got a dreadful jolt when we went into that creepy cottage. Been having nightmares ever since. Hasn't got my strong nerves, you see. I had nursing experience in the War so I kept my head better!'

'Quite so, quite so!' Rev. Valentine smiled warmly at his parishioners. 'Well, delighted to meet you all, and I trust we will see you at the ceremony next week? Two o'clock, Thursday, in the church?'

Everybody rewarded him with nods and smiles of agreement. Phoebe promised that she and Celia would produce some floral decorations in honour of Gladys and Elfrida.

The Reverend thanked them, and remarked on the unusually busy week ahead. 'Dorothy and I have to go now. You see, our maid Ruby's over at Wood Hall helping them get the place spruced up ready for the cocktail party on Saturday. We were happy to oblige, of course. But without Ruby, Dorothy's even busier than usual.'

'Oh yes, the cocktail party!' said Celia. She turned to Svetla and Ivan. 'I suppose it's all go down at Wood Hall just now, with Miss Hepzibah's special day looming. Must say it's an age since I visited the old girl.'

'Yes – in fact we must be getting back, Cook wants these blackberries for some jam tarts for Saturday', said Svetla. 'And me and Ivan have to wash all those huge windows this afternoon.'

'I suppose I'm normally one of the only visitors Miss Hamilton-Tracy ever sees these days,' commented the Vicar. 'I pop in from time to time, just to see how the old lady is. I'm afraid her home strikes me as rather chilly and dismal. All those huge empty rooms! I must say, her Cook always brings me a few delightful cakes – also 'the cup that cheers, but does not inebriate.' Noticing the puzzled expressions on the faces of Ivan and Svetla, he added 'I mean, a nice cup of tea!'

Phoebe remarked that her husband Walter, the doctor, also visited from time to time. 'Only the Cook, Mary Anne the housemaid, and that poor frail old Hepzibah rattling about in the place these days.' She turned to Ivan and Svetla. 'You two live in a flat above the old racing stables, don't you?'

'That's right,' replied Ivan. 'But there's visitors staying in Hall now, Basil and Amelia Bantam-Cox. This party's Madam Amelia's idea of course. So we're all running rings around place, trying to make it more welcoming.'

Svetla pulled a face. 'Yes, it's hard work. I like to work peacefully in garden, and Ivan sees to grounds. There's no horses for him to look after now, that's what he always loved best.'

Dorothy was sympathetic. 'I suppose it's all hands on deck, dusting and tidying and scrubbing, getting the place up to scratch. Our Ruby says she's never worked so hard in her life, poor girl. But a ninetieth birthday is something special, we're all looking forward to the party, aren't we, Bertram dear?'

Her husband agreed, took Dorothy's arm, and made apologies for leaving. 'I'm afraid we must go, duty calls, you know. So good to see you all. Come along now, Dorothy. So very kind of you ladies to help with the flowers.'

Ivan and Svetla, their basket overflowing with fruit, set off in the opposite direction, down to the water meadows and woodlands that surrounded Wood Hall. Celia and Phoebe were left discussing plans for Thursday; one would bring chrysanthemums, the other Michaelmas Daisies and Golden Rod.

As they set off towards their homes, Maude and Colonel Mortimer rounded the corner.

'What ho, old girl!' boomed Mortimer, spotting Celia. Maude had little Dotty firmly on a lead, panting and half-choking on her collar in attempts to reach Celia and Phoebe. Mortimer and Maude were both speaking at once.

'….just been chatting with Svetla and Ivan. Told us some rum stuff about gathering poisonous mushrooms in Bohemia when they were little 'uns…'

'…….amazing stuff, that Fly whatsit! Seems it's collected by the ton in Lapland! Reindeer herdsmen, Ivan says!'

'Whatever are you gabbling about?' demanded Celia.

Her husband paused to get his breath 'Seems the Laplanders pile the stuff on the ground when they want to round up the herds. Reindeer can't get enough of that fungus. If a herd's running free and they need to round 'em up, down go the baskets of Agaric and up gallop the reindeer!'

'Wish I could get my Dotty trained to come like that!' exclaimed Maude, fondling her little dog's head as she spoke.

The Colonel continued. 'The beasts stampede to get at the stuff, gives them a kind of thrill, like champers to us at parties! They go mad for it!'

Maude gave a snort of laughter. 'Maybe we'll have poison mushroom over at the Wood Hall cocktail bash! That'd liven old Hepzibah up!'

The Colonel grinned down at his wife's Aunt. 'Good idea, Maudie! That'd be something different. Apparently it sets people off dancing like whirling dervishes!'

'And do you know,' said Maude with relish, 'that pathologist even tested that poor dead moggy. Old cat had traces of poison mushroom in his tum. I suppose he jumped on the table to get a share of the fish, after the old witches had passed out cold!'

Phoebe was shocked and quite taken aback by Maude's coarse and rather heartless reference to the Pentelows. She remarked in disapproving tones 'We should be glad at least, that those two poor old ladies passed away without pain. Walter thinks they probably collapsed and died quite quickly. That's one blessing.'

The Colonel was ready to go. 'Well, must get on. Goodbye, Phoebe, see you at old Hepzibah's bash. Come along, Maude, and you, Celia. Chap gets a bit peckish this time of day, you know!' Pipe in mouth, he stomped off.

Maude lingered. 'That old trout Hepzibah's a bit far gone, y'know. Wonder if she even knows she's going to be ninety? They say she's in bed most of the day. I bet she doesn't know her arse from her elbow these days!'

Phoebe's response was faint; she was offended by Maude's vulgarity. 'Is that so? But everyone's looking forward to the party.'

Celia agreed. 'Yes, should be a good party. They say old Miss Hepzibah's a wealthy woman, and that niece of hers, Amelia, has a free hand with the catering. Between ourselves, I think Amelia and her husband.... Basil, I think it is..... are gold diggers. After all, they turn up out of the blue, when the old lady's losing her marbles, move into free lodgings, and grab hold of the purse strings!'

Maude nodded in agreement. 'Still, nothing like a good knees-up, I always say. Super! Well, cheerio, Phoebe, see you at the funeral.' And with that, Maude and Celia hurried off in the direction of The Gables, in the wake of the starving Mortimer.

THREE – SATURDAY MORNING AT WOOD HALL

The huge beamed kitchen at Wood Hall was a hive of industry that Saturday. Mabel, the Ponsonby's maid, had joined Ruby, Mary Anne and the stout old Cook, in a frantic effort to prepare for the first party Wood Hall had seen for many a year. The long table held a variety of plates, mostly remnants of Victorian flowered dinner services. On these, they were arranging tasty tidbits of party goodies. Cook, her face florid from heat and activity, stood up to ease her aching back, pushed her wispy hair out of her eyes, and surveyed the scene with satisfaction.

'Well, I must say it's a nice change 'avin' someone to talk to!' she said, to the room in general. Her three helpers paused, and Mary Anne, who had lived and worked at Wood Hall almost as long as Cook herself, answered.

'Yes, very chummy. Us'lly I'm all on me own, sweepin' and dustin' this spooky ol' place, and runnin' in an' out after old Miss 'amilton-Tracy. Not that she can 'elp it, poor ol' soul. She can't even sit up wivout I 'elps 'er.'

Young Ruby spoke up. 'Miss 'epzibah 'amilton-Tracy! My, that's a mouthful, ain't it?'

Cook explained in hushed tones. 'Between ourselves, Mary Anne 'n' me, we calls 'er Miss H-T. But Gawd 'elp us if we ever let 'er 'ear us! She always were a right stickler fer ev'ry thin' done right 'n' proper!'

Mabel stood up straight, hands on hips, and regarded her companions. 'An' now you'm got that there Amelia, and 'er feller Basil 'ere, expectin' you to wait on them as well!'

Cook scratched her head thoughtfully. 'Yes. An' I don't reckon as Miss H-T were too pleased to see 'em, neither! I often 'eard 'er say 'ow as that Amelia were a baggage, a right barrel o' mischief, when she stayed 'ere as a kiddie. Amelia's Mum were Miss H-T's younger sister, yer see.'

Ruby warmed to the theme. 'Amelia don't 'alf give 'erself airs. An' I seen 'er creepin' all round 'er Aunt. "How are yer today, Aunt 'epzibah dear? Are yer comfy in yer bed? Shall I plump up yer pillas a bit for yer?" On an' on she goes!'

Mary Anne chuckled. 'You got it right there, Ruby! Miss H-T were quite sharp wiv 'er yesterd'y. I 'eard 'er say "Fer goodness sake, Amelia, can't yer find summat to do and give me a bit o' peace? Why don't you and that 'usband o' yours go fer a walk round the lake, or in the woods, an' get some fresh air! Get Ivan to saddle you a coupla 'osses and go fer a ride!"'

Cook smiled wryly. 'That's a joke! No 'osses in this place fer nigh on fifteen year. Old Miss H-T, she lives in the past a lot o' the time now, poor ol' soul.'

Mabel now spoke confidentially. 'Talkin' of 'osses…. I reckon that Mr.

Basil's got a problem gamblin' on 'em. Twice, I was near the front 'all an' I 'eard 'im usin' the phone. And that Amelia really went fer 'im. She were right angry. "What yer doin', yer barmy idiot?" I 'eard 'er say. "Yer knows we're in trouble wiv the bank already. We ain't got no money to bet on the 'osses no more!" Or summat like that.'

Cook sniffed loudly before speaking. 'Well, I must say, she's a fine one to talk! Three times I've caught 'er at the drinks cupboard, 'elpin' 'erself. An' she looks right flushed an' doo-lally sometimes, y'know. Both got expensive tastes an' no money to pay fer 'em, I reckon. Well, come on, girls. 'Ave a look in the range, Mary Anne, see if it needs stokin' up. Ain't that pastry ready yet, Ruby?'

The door opened as she finished speaking, and in rushed Amelia, looking flushed and anxious. She looked all of her age, Cook thought to herself, when she was upset or worried. Cook struggled with some mental arithmetic and came to the conclusion that Amelia must now be in her mid-thirties. In Cook's opinion, her skirts were too short, her neck-lines too plunging. She had adopted some of the modern flapper styles of dress but had never let her lustrous black curls be styled into a fashionable bob. Cook had a theory that this was so that she could toss it back from her face as she flounced and flaunted her wares whenever men were present. But still, Cook had a soft spot for Amelia.

Amelia now addressed Cook in a voice full of tension. 'Cook, may I have a word, please? We've got a new house guest, just arrived! It's my cousin Charles, from Kenya!'

Cook's ruddy face broke into a broad smile. 'Charlie! That young rascal! Not seen 'im fer donkey's years! Where is 'e, then?'

There was no smile on Amelia's face as she replied. 'He's in with Aunt Hepzibah. Seems he knew her ninetieth birthday was coming up, so he made a surprise visit home to congratulate her.'

What was the matter with the girl? Thought Cook. The two had been as thick as thieves in the old days. Now Amelia looked as if she had seen a ghost. 'Are you all right, Miss Amelia?' she enquired kindly. 'Yer lookin' a bit pale an' shaky. 'Ere, sit down a minute, I'll mek yer a cup o' tea.'

Amelia sank gratefully into the cushioned chair Cook pulled out for her, and wiped a weary hand across her forehead. She looked dejected and downcast; her voice shook. 'Thank you, Cook. You always were so good to me. It's just the shock of seeing Charles again so unexpectedly, you know.'

Cook smiled as she remembered past days, when the two small cousins played hide and seek in the cavernous rooms and corridors, and got up to mischief in the woods and parkland together. Always climbing trees, pestering Ivan for a ride on the fine horses. Rowing in the lake and coming in soaked to the skin.

'You two was great mates as kiddies, weren't yer? Yer must've missed 'im these last years. Though as I recalls, you went off to Kenya as well, all those years ago. Isn't that right? You was a governess or summat, out there?'

Amelia's voice was small and uncertain as she responded. 'That's right, but the heat didn't agree with me. Then my father needed me after my mother died. He was very unwell, some liver problem. So I came home again.'

'Then I 'eard,' went on Cook, 'after yer Dad died, your old place were all sold up, weren't it?'

These memories were obviously painful for Amelia and at first she struggled to answer. Then she looked tremulously up at Cook. 'Yes. It was a terrible time, very hard. Aunt Hepzibah helped me find somewhere to live.'

Cook passed her a cup of tea, saying 'Down in 'ampshire, weren't it?'

'Yes, I went as companion to Auntie's old school friend. That's where I met dear Basil, of course. He came as house guest one summer.'

'Then we 'eard as you was married!'

'That's right,' replied Amelia in a subdued, uncertain voice. 'I married Basil.'

The three maids had been working in complete silence in order not to miss a word of the conversation. Now Mary Anne stepped forward and asked Amelia whether she should prepare a room for Mr. Charles.

Amelia seemed to pull herself together with an effort, before replying. 'Yes. Charles likes the Blue Room. That's where he always slept when we were children. I….I'd better go and talk to Charles, and see how Aunt Hepzibah is. She's not used to surprise visitors these days.'

Setting down her tea cup, Amelia stood up and made purposefully for the door. The four women watched her go, then closed the door and exchanged glances.

Cook shook her head in bewilderment. 'Well! Madam's in a right state, and no mistake! She 'asn't even drunk 'er cup o' tea. She 'n young Master Charles was thick as thieves when they was littl'uns, always up to summat together. Used to sneak in 'ere and raid me biscuit tin, as I recalls only too well. Cheeky little beggars!'

Mary Anne asked 'Shall I tek a tray o' tea into Miss H-T's room, with an extra cup fer Mr. Charles, then?'

Mabel got busy preparing a tea tray, saying 'I'll do that for yer, Mary, seein' as you've the bedroom to get ready an' all.'

Ruby was equally keen to help, offering to work upstairs with Mary Anne.

'I'll 'elp yer clean out that big ol' bedroom, Mary Anne. I s'pose we ought to warm the bed an' ev'rythin'.'

All three were soon busy elsewhere, so Cook worked on alone at her jam tarts, vol-au-vents, pigs-in-blankets and tiny iced cakes for the party. Half an hour went by before the kitchen door opened again. There stood Amelia in her outdoor jacket and gumboots, a determined gleam in her dark eyes.

'Cook, I need to go out for a breath of fresh air. I'll just have a little stroll in the woods. I'll help you get things ready for the party when I get back. The guests won't arrive for two or three hours. I'd like to help, you know. Maybe I could mix the fruit punch for you? I'm good at that.'

Cook was startled by this offer from unexpected quarters. 'It's all right, Madam, I'm sure I can manage, don't you fret!'

'But I'd like to help if I can! Help make Auntie's party a bit special. After all, it was my idea, you know. I'll be back soon. Leave the punch for me to do please, Cook.'

So saying, she selected a basket from a row hanging on nails behind the back door, and was off.

'Well I never!' muttered Cook under her breath. 'Wonders never cease, they say! Never knew that minx to 'elp anyone in 'er life before! An' it ain't even April Fools' Day.'

FOUR – THE COCKTAIL PARTY

There was a lively buzz of conversation in the long drawing room that evening. Mary Anne had lit a log fire in the massive open hearth. The unswept chimney caused wisps of smoke to drift into the room; the guests had therefore retreated to the far end, near the French windows. Cook's tasty nibbles were already finding favour with the gaily-dressed company, who stood in a small group, glasses in hand.

Amelia had Basil by the arm and was introducing him. Basil felt embarrassed and uncomfortable under the scrutiny of these strangers. He had made a life-long study of the art of sliding un-noticed around the edges of large groups of guests in the homes of various distant acquaintances. He tried to give the impression of having arrived with someone more closely acquainted with the hosts, hoping no-one would spot him making free with the available food and drink. Now, here he was, exposed, with just a handful of people who all knew each other, and who seemed to be eying him from head to toe, with distinctly disdainful expressions. Lord knew what they were all thinking!

This evening, Basil wore a greeny-brown suit with a grid of red lines, which did nothing to enhance his short bulky form. His only dress-suit had suffered a dire accident involving a full gravy jug at the last party he had attended. Under his jacket (a throw-out from an acquaintance), Basil wore a striped shirt. A red bow tie showed under his series of clean-shaven double chins. He was horribly conscious of looking like a cross between a circus clown and a seedy race-course bookie. His nerves were in pieces. He had searched the house for cigarettes. Sometimes he had been lucky enough to discover some on the kitchen mantelpiece, taking just a couple so that Cook might not notice. But today, he had found nothing.

Basil had oiled his sparse remaining hair, which he allowed to grow longer on the left side than on the right. This was to enable him to comb some long greasy strands over his shiny bald pate. This worked well unless he became too animated, when the longest hairs tended to fall back and hang down almost to his left shoulder, to Amelia's considerable annoyance. She had told him in no uncertain terms to keep his head as still as possible. This caused him to walk with peculiar stiffness, and to stare straight ahead like a portly guard on duty.

After she had made a tour of the room, presenting Basil to all the neighbours, Amelia repeated the tour with Charles, her cousin, whom few of them had met before. Courteous words were exchanged as guests surveyed each other curiously.

As Amelia introduced Charles to Reverend Valentine and his wife with the words '…and this is my cousin, Charles, over here from Kenya,' Dorothy was sure she heard the charming, dapper Charles mutter angrily under his breath. The words were 'Cousin, yes… among other things!'

Aloud, he said politely 'Yes, I'm Amelia's cousin, home from Kenya on a nostalgic trip to help celebrate Aunt Hepzibah's birthday. Delighted to meet you.'

Mortimer, while leaning across the table for another handful of delicious 'Devils on horseback', glanced through the French windows and noticed three figures stomping around the lawns, peering closely at the flower borders in the gathering dusk. Was that Aunt Maude? And surely, that was Phoebe Jones, stumbling awkwardly in her high heels? He could not discern whether the third person was male or female. Whatever were they doing out there? Mortimer felt irritated and wondered whether he might open the door unobserved and tell the wandering guests to come inside and join the party, like any well-behaved guest should. Instead, he pointed them out to Celia, who shrugged her shoulders helplessly. Old Maudie was not easy to bring to heel.

Amelia seemed determined to assist the maids in the task of making guests feel at home and enjoy themselves. Periodically she was observed fetching the large glass jug of fruit punch from the long table, and doing the rounds of the guests, insisting on topping up their glasses. When she popped out to the kitchen for further supplies, Charles used her absence to corner Basil. Celia overheard a conversation between them, and nudged her husband in the ribs to make him listen. She was fascinated by Charles, who was dark and handsome, with an air of authority which stemmed from long years of giving orders and making decisions on the tea plantation.

'So, you're Amelia's new husband, Basil Bantam-Cox, I understand,' said Charles, fixing the nervous Basil with a gimlet-like stare.

Basil touched his head awkwardly before replying. Was his hair behaving, or was it becoming ridiculously lop-sided? Why was this cocksure cousin of his wife staring at him so intently? Basil cleared his throat, and swallowed hard.

'Well ….. not really a new husband exactly… we've been married more than four years now. Just came over to wish the old gal well on her birthday, don't you know,' he replied, chortling foolishly.

Celia, thinking to ease a tense situation, inserted herself between the two gentlemen, saying brightly 'Well, Basil…. and Charles ….I'm sure you'll both get on splendidly in our little village. We'll have to introduce you to all the gang…. all great chums, great chums!' She waved her arm expansively, to include all present company as 'chums'. She then addressed Charles again, fluttering her lashes in what she hoped was a coyly attractive manner. 'Do you have a wife, Charles, or are you a bachelor gay?'

Charles appeared not to know the answer to this straight-forward question. He looked angry and confused, and was only rescued by the noisy arrival of Maude, with Phoebe in tow.

The Colonel, always keen to share memories and views with other ex-Colonial chaps, wandered over, asking 'So, I gather you've come over from Kenya, Charles? Tea plantation, you say?

Charles explained that he had worked his way up over the years to his present position of Plantation Manager. 'Good life out there, you know, plenty of sun.'

'Plenty of sun, yes!' agreed the Colonel heartily. 'Like in India. Fellow has to escape to the hills in the hot season, don't y'know!'

Basil escaped forlornly to the table in search of more punch, finding and drinking a half-full glass someone else had set down, since the jug was missing. He had to steady his nerves somehow. When he had first met Amelia, he had clung to her like a drowning man. His own parents had sunk into poverty and disrepute through a lethal mix of gambling and alcohol. When Amelia spoke to him about being an heiress, her childless Aunt living in a huge mansion in Suffolk, hope had sprung in his heart. Only gradually had he begun to understand that Amelia's need for him sprang from the difficulties faced by a penniless single woman approaching middle-age, when trying to be accepted socially.

Now here they both were, in this dilapidated and depressing mansion, no race-course nearer than Newmarket, and the bright lights far away… He had smuggled a half-bottle of Hepzibah's whiskey upstairs to give himself and Amelia 'Dutch courage' before the ordeal of the party. To his surprise, she had refused to drink with him so he had downed the whole bottle himself. In fact, Amelia had been strangely elusive all afternoon and he felt terribly vulnerable and alone.

Basil's reverie was interrupted by the raucous voice of an elderly, dumpy woman in muddy brogues appearing at his elbow.

'Isn't this jolly? Hallo, I'm told you are Amelia's husband, Mr. Bantam-Cox! So sorry we're a bit on the drag!'

A prim-looking woman with tightly-rolled hair pinned each side of her head, like a pair of headphones, now stepped forward, explaining that she was Phoebe Jones, wife of the local Doctor, who had been suddenly called to an emergency so had left her to walk the long avenue of limes leading to Wood Hall, alone. 'And when I at last reached the front entrance, Svetla insisted on showing me all around the grounds before I could come in!'

'New herbaceous borders, most attractive!' boomed Maude.

Charles appeared beside the two newcomers, saying 'The grounds are a full-time job for Svetla and Ivan. When I was a boy there was a team of gardeners here, and those two just cared for the stables. No teams of gardeners around here now. Money's a bit tight these days.'

Maude called loudly across the room to the Colonel. 'What ho, Mortimer! Are you going to introduce us properly please?'

The Colonel strode towards them. 'Righto.... Charles, this is Maude, my wife's Aunt. Maude, this is Charles Hamilton-Tracy, Amelia's cousin. And this is Phoebe Jones, the Doctor's good lady!'

Maude gazed closely at Charles, before remarking 'Amelia's cousin Charles.... Now I can see who you are! Always over here as a kiddie, getting into scrapes with Amelia, I remember!'

Celia broke in to explain 'And this is Mr. Basil Bantam-Cox, Amelia's husband.'

The greetings and hand-shakings were interrupted by a loud announcement from Amelia, returning with the large glass jug newly filled with fruit punch.

'Fruit punch, anyone? Very refreshing, especially the slices of orange and cucumber, I always think. Do let me fill up your glasses.' She proceeded to circulate, not content until all glasses were re-filled. She then surveyed the room with satisfaction. 'Good! Now I'll just go and see if dear Aunt Hepzibah's all right. After all, this is her birthday.'

Dorothy and the Vicar were admiring all the fancy food on the long table. Dorothy took a bite out of a vol-au-vent, before turning to her husband. 'Bertram dear, do try one of these little pastry things – look, they have prawns in them, and I believe this tasty sauce must be mushroom.'

The Vicar popped a whole one in his mouth, saying 'Quite right, my dear, they are delicious.'

'I've never tasted anything quite like this fruit punch before,' continued his wife. 'It's spicy and most refreshing.' She finished her drink, then said uncertainly 'Oh dear, I think I need to sit down.' Unsteadily, she sank into a chair. 'My head's sort of swimmy... I...I feel rather strange.'

The Vicar swayed slightly as he turned to look at his wife. 'Shwimmy, did you shay, dearesht?' Staggering slightly, he moved to lean against a wall. Something odd seemed to have happened to his eyes. Looking vaguely across the room, he caught sight of Mabel and Ruby, entering the room with more trays of nibbles. They wore white frilly blouses, short black skirts, dainty little white aprons and charming frilly head bands.

'Good God!' he muttered to himself, 'are those Chorus Girls?' He gazed around the room; everything seemed to be in motion, and bright colours shimmered everywhere. The conversations around him became a meaningless deafening buzz.

Celia, finding the punch had gone straight to her head, had sunk onto a shabby settee and was laughing wildly at nothing in particular. Her husband the esteemed Colonel was shambling crabwise across the worn flowered carpet towards Ruby and Mabel, his mouth falling foolishly open, his eyes bulging.

Basil and Charles were both wobbly on their feet, both in process of emptying their glasses and looking for something to lean on.

Maude and Phoebe, who had only recently joined the party, were mesmerised by the behaviour of their fellow guests.

When Amelia entered the room with yet more punch, saying it was really time to drink a little toast to Auntie, Maude made a bee-line for her, saying 'By golly, Amelia, that punch is just the ticket! Phoebe and I have missed out rather, coming late! I love a little tipple!'

Amelia was glad to oblige, and re-filled Maude's glass. But Phoebe, looking around at the foolishly grinning guests, hastily moved her glass out of reach, saying 'No thank you, Amelia, I'm really not used to strong drink, in fact it makes me rather ill.'

'Nonsense!' said Amelia, filling Phoebe's glass to the brim. 'We must all get in the party spirit for Auntie's ninetieth! After all, getting to ninety is quite and achievement!'

With that, she began to fill every glass in sight with a kind of grim determination. When she flounced out of the room, her jug empty, Phoebe walked over to the Colonel, who was towering over Mabel to whom he was singing some unintelligible song. He gladly took Phoebe's glass and downed its contents.

Amid this extraordinary noise and confusion, the door opened and in walked Sir John and Lady Imogen, dressed to the nines for the occasion. Sir John stopped short in mid-sentence (he was making apologies for late arrival due to delay at the Magistrates' Court) and gazed in amazement at the scene before him. His lady wife was horror-struck at the undignified behaviour of her friends. Could she really believe the evidence of her eyes and ears?

The Vicar and the Colonel were giggling foolishly, slopping drink around and exchanging the most dubious jokes. 'That hit'th the thpot.... ath the actreth thaid to the Bith... Bithp... Bithop!'

Surely that was not the Vicar's voice? Lady Imogen spun round to see that yes, it was; the Colonel and dear Bertram were giving each other friendly wild slaps on the back which nearly had them both down on the floor.

Basil was already on the floor, giving a drunken rendering of 'Roll along home', while in the far corner (Lady Imogen could hardly believe her eyes!) Dorothy and Celia seemed to be engaged in a feeble fight. The words 'Do'thy dear, I do b'lieve you've put on weight, you're a podgy piggy!' were audible as Celia poked her friend in the stomach. Dorothy retaliated by grabbing a handful of Celia's hair with the words 'Well, your hair'th a dithgrathe! It's a ridicluth meth, you look like a thcarecrow!' The two then subsided into giggles, clutching each other before stumbling against the table, where Celia grabbed a tray of small iced cakes. Together they flopped down onto a pouffe by the hearth, where they gobbled the food down between helpless giggles.

In the centre of the room, Charles suddenly lunged towards the prostrate Basil shouting 'Huthband, ith it, Bathil? Good mind to punch you in the fathe!' Attempting to hit Basil, Charles instead rolled onto the floor on top of him. Wild thumps and kicks were noisily exchanged; Basil was being badly battered. Sir John grabbed the two helpless combatants, trying to pull them apart with the words 'Gentlemen! Please, try to behave like gentlemen!' He then gazed in astonishment at the long mousy locks which now hung down over Basil's left shoulder. Extraordinary!

Meanwhile the Vicar had grabbed hold of Ruby, gabbling 'I jutht love thethe little unith….uni…frilly thingamabobs!' Oblivious to her squeals of 'Stop it, Vicar, yer ticklin' me, yer messin' up me 'air, leave go of me!' he was holding on tight.

The Colonel had Mabel on his lap. She was wriggling like an eel, shouting 'Let me go, get yer big 'ands orf of me! I'll tell my Sam of yer!'

'You're a grand bukthm wench! Natty outfit, what!' gloated the Colonel, continuing to fondle her freely. Finally Sir John, appalled beyond endurance, threw the contents of a water jug over both would-be Romeos enabling the two blushing and offended maids to escape and make for the door.

As the dishevelled girls disappeared towards the kitchen, gasping and protesting loudly, Amelia entered with another plate of vol-au-vents, saying gleefully 'I thought we needed a bit more food to go with the drink! I'm afraid some of our guests have rather over-indulged.'

Lady Imogen and Phoebe sat stiffly either side of Maude on a long settee, refusing to let her get up in search of another drink. They watched in stunned silence as Amelia bent down over the almost comatose Charles on the floor.

'Open wide, Charles! In it goes!' She thrust a handful of vol-au-vents into his slack mouth. Basil reached across to help himself from the plate.

'No no, Basil! Remember what the doctor said to you about rich food!' cried Amelia, snatching away the plate and making a hasty exit, followed by Basil's violent protests. He struggled to get up, but slumped down again helplessly.

Charles, choking and grimacing, removed the unwanted food from his mouth and dropped it into an empty glass with the words 'Thrimpth! Dithguth... nathty thingth, can't thtand theafood!'

Things seemed to be calming down at last. Sir John helped the disconsolate Colonel and the bewildered Reverend gentleman onto armchairs, with instructions for them to 'Have a little rest, pull yourselves together, then go straight home.'

Amelia entered as order was being restored. In a rather shrill, hysterical voice she announced 'I've just been in to see Auntie, and she's sitting up, ready to hear us sing to her. Her door's wide open. Come on, all of you, let's sing Happy Birthday!'

During the appalling tuneless rendering that followed, a woman in a highly emotional state, wearing a fur cape and carrying a small suitcase, burst unannounced into the room. She gazed around, mystified by the slumped figures, some of whom were singing tunelessly, others stuffing food into their mouths. The Vicar had his arm around his giggling wife and was nuzzling her ear. Celia was at the table, stuffing her handbag with goodies. Maude was loudly resisting the attentions of her grim lady jailers. Lady Imogen was complaining 'Has everyone taken leave of their senses? Really, this is too much'.

Suddenly the newcomer shrieked in horror, dropping her suitcase with a thud. Her eyes were fixed on the two men still wrestling feebly on the carpet while uttering a stream of garbled insults.

'Charles!' she screamed. 'Are you all right? I've been looking everywhere for you!'

Charles managed to open first one eye, then the other. He was suddenly alert and still, gazing at her in disbelief. She fell to her knees beside him, took his flushed face in her hands and kissed him passionately on the mouth. 'Whatever are you doing down on the floor? Are you all right, my darling?'

Her hat fell off revealing wavy blond locks (bottle blond, surmised Lady Imogen). Charles struggled to a sitting position and flung his arms around her with the words 'Candida! Oh, Candida my love! However did you find me?'

FIVE – AN EVENING OF SUPRISES

In the kitchen, when all the guests were gone, Mary Anne was busy piling up plates. In the old armchair, Cook lay back fast asleep, snoring heavily. On a bench by the wall sat Candida, as if frozen, stunned and silent after her strange experiences.

Unsteady footsteps sounded on the uneven flagstones of the passage, and Basil entered the kitchen. His clothing was rumpled, his bow tie awry, but his hair was now correctly in place. He was carrying a plate holding three small vol-au-vents. He looked weary, and a trifle dazed. 'Where is everyone?' he asked, looking around the vast kitchen. Seeing Candida sitting on the bench, he proffered the plate, saying 'Do help yourself, Madam'.

Candida shook her head, and replied in a faint, shaky voice. 'No thank you, I couldn't eat a thing. I just don't understand what's going on. It took me ages to find out where Charles was, and I thought he'd be really pleased to see me.'

Basil regarded her. 'Yes, you're his fiancée, I understand. Congratulations. Candida, isn't it?'

'That's right', said Candida plaintively. 'But Charles is behaving so strangely, and now, he's disappeared. And here I am, on my own in this dreary old mansion, and nobody explains anything to me! I just feel so tired and lost and confused.'

Basil sat down heavily on the bench beside her. 'Yes, that was one weird party. I just couldn't work out what was going on. Can't remember much now…. but everybody seemed very wound up and touchy and that fruit punch went straight to my head.'

Mary Anne carried a heavy load of plates to the sink, then turned to face Basil. 'Are you all right, Mr. Basil, Sir? You look a bit feverish.'

Basil brushed his hand wearily across his forehead, a puzzled look on his round face. 'Well, I do feel a bit odd. I went into Miss Hepzibah's room to say goodnight, but she was asleep, snoring like the dickens. Then I fell asleep in her armchair. And now there's hardly anyone around.'

Mary Anne stood with her hand on her hip, looking scornful at the memory.

'They've all gone home, Mr. Basil, and not before time! Never 'eard such a racket! Talk about respectin' our betters! I couldn't believe me eyes when I saw the mess they made!'

Basil looked around the large kitchen. 'Where's my wife? Thought she must be in here.'

Mary Anne looked thoughtful. 'Well, she was 'ere. Then she went out, to the lake, with Mr. Charles… 'e wasn't quite 'imself some'ow…. And Madam was only wearin' that flimsy party frock. She must be fruzz to the marrer stayin' out all this time.'

'That's rum,' commented Basil. 'I'll go and look for her when I've eaten this lot.' He ate the last three vol-au-vents, and passed the plate to Mary Anne, with 'Here's another plate for you to wash up, Mary Anne…. found it on that tall chest in Auntie's room just now, when I woke up.'

'Righto, give it 'ere, Sir,' said the long-suffering Mary Anne, adding it to the pile in the shallow stone sink. She turned her back on the plates and rested her elbows on the rim of the sink, glad to have someone to chat to. Basil was licking his lips contentedly. 'Those little pastry thingies are quite tasty…. bits of crab mixed in sauce, I think. Some kind of seafood, anyway. What's the matter with Cook?'

Mary Anne shrugged her shoulders helplessly. ''Eaven knows! I come in 'ere…I'd bin settlin' down Miss 'epzibah… an' there were Cook, out cold on that there chair. Couldn't wake 'er up! Ruby and Mabel, they's gone 'ome in a fit o' the sulks. Said as they weren't never comin' back to this mad'ouse!'

'I know how they feel!' said Basil meaningfully. 'How long ago did my wife and that cousin of hers go outside, would you say?'

'Oh… nearly a 'alf hour, I'd say. I 'eard 'em say they was goin' down to the lake, tryin' to clear their 'eads a bit. But it's right dark out there.'

Candida was obviously distressed. 'What can they be doing out there?'

Basil scowled. 'Yes, what can they be doing? It's late, and there's no moon even, all clouded over. Whatever are they thinking? I don't trust that toffee-nosed chap Charles an inch, somehow.'

Candida became angry, crying 'Don't talk like that about my Charles!' Basil was taken aback. 'Oh, sorry! No offence, I hope. It's been a bad day for me. Had some business deals to do, really thought this one was a winner. Phoned my broker, and its all gone up the spout again.' Basil rubbed his face, shaking his head and twitching slightly. 'Blow me, whatever was in that punch? Extraordinary stuff! My head's still reeling. Think I'll go out and get some fresh air too. I'll walk down to the lake, see if I can find my wife.'

So saying, Basil walked unsteadily to the back door and disappeared into the night.

Mary Anne watched him go, her expression sceptical. 'Huh! Business deals, 'e calls it. It's just bettin'…. 'orse racin'. I 'eard 'im on the phone. I 'eard 'im say "Fell at the first fence? The devil 'e did! I've bin swindled, they said 'e was a sure-fire winner!" Then he thumped that phone down nigh on 'ard enough to break it, and stomped upstairs.'

Getting no response from Candida, Mary Anne squeezed out a dish cloth and set to work wiping the table. After a few moments, the back door opened, and in walked Charles, staggering slightly. He sat down heavily on one of the wooden chairs that stood around the table. Sighing heavily, he buried his face in his hands, his shoulders slumped. He had seemed not to notice Candida's presence. She now stood up, and walked quietly over to him, tentatively taking his hand in hers. Charles raised his head, anxiously surveying his fiancée. Finally he spoke. 'Thank you, my darling. I'm sorry I've neglected you. It's been a strange day and I had a lot to think about. And I felt so confused and wobbly all evening. You can have my bed tonight, I'll sleep down here somewhere.'

For answer, Candida tenderly placed a kiss on his cheek, smiling uncertainly.

The spell was broken as Cook snored even louder, like some lumbering rhinoceros. Charles turned to look at her with curiosity. 'What's the matter with Cook? She's snoring like a grumpus!'

Mary Anne left the dishes and walked over to shake Cook's shoulder. 'I dunno. Evr'ythin's gone crazy ternight.'

Cook suddenly straightened up, rubbed her eyes, and looked around the kitchen as if she couldn't believe her eyes. Then, to the astonishment of three mesmerised witnesses, she leaped from her chair and started to dance. She seemed to be attempting something resembling a hornpipe. Croakily, she started to sing.

'What shall we do with the drunken sailor…early in the mornin'!'
This was too much for Candida. She clung to Charles. 'Charles, I'm scared! Everyone here is so very odd, and I feel as if I'm in a bad dream.'

Charles looked at her tenderly. 'It's not usually like this, sweetheart, honestly! Sit down, don't get upset, it will all go back to normal I'm sure.' Settling Candida on a chair, Charles approached the frantically twirling Cook. 'Cook, are you all right?'

Without warning, Cook grabbed Charles by both hands, stumbling as she tried to involve him in her mad dance. Charles extracted himself with difficulty, and returned to Candida's side. Cook's singing became more raucous. Mary Anne was wordlessly staring at her old companion, then she too sat down, unequal to the extraordinary change in Cook's usually dour demeanour.

Suddenly, the outer door opened, and in burst Amelia, a shawl around her shoulders. She gazed astounded at Cook's antics, then turned and saw Candida and Charles at the table.

A terrified scream came from Amelia. She stumbled back, her face ashen.

'No! It can't be you, Charles! It's a ghost! Help! Charles…. But Charles is at the bottom of the lake! And where's my Basil?' She staggered slightly before falling to the floor in a faint.

Charles sat stunned. Cook subsided, exhausted, into her armchair, and closed her eyes. Mary Anne rushed for the door to the corridor, wailing 'That settles it! I'm 'andin' in me notice!'

SIX – REVELATIONS

The following day, Sunday, held a surprise for some of the good people of Meadowford who arrived at St. Mildred's to discover only the organist and one churchwarden in charge. Mr. Mayes the People's Warden announced that the Vicar was indisposed, but would probably be recovered in time to conduct Evensong. Since many of the choir were also unaccountably absent, Mr. Crouch the organist agreed to play hymns chosen by members of the small congregation.

After several favourites had been sung, the congregation went happily home, busily speculating on possible reasons for this strange state of affairs. Many of them had noticed Constable Black riding around the village lanes on his bike, in his uniform, and some had also seen the gleaming automobile of Inspector Sharpe weaving through the lanes. Everywhere, tongues were wagging.

Meanwhile at Wood Hall, Doctor Walter Jones, and police personnel including Plain Clothes Officers, were fully occupied. Sleepy Meadowford Magna had rarely seen so many cars, nor heard so many flying rumours. An Officer stood at each Gate Lodge of Wood Hall to repel nosey parkers.

In the drawing room of Wood Hall, scene of yesterday's party, a circle of chairs had been drawn up. The long table had been pushed to one side, and from behind it Inspector Sharpe faced an audience of witnesses (or were they suspects?)

Svetla, Ivan, Sir John Greenwood and his lady wife, Celia, Maude, Colonel Blunkett, Phoebe, Candida, Charles, Amelia, Cook, Mary Anne, Mabel and Ruby sat in tense silence. Many of them looked distinctly under the weather and ill at ease as they waited for the Inspector to speak. Constable Black sat beside the Inspector, looking alert and excited, pencil and notepad at the ready. The Inspector opened proceedings.

'Thank you all, ladies and gentlemen, for coming so promptly. Reverend Valentine and his wife have sent word that they will arrive as soon as they can. I believe…' (he paused to cough discreetly)… 'they are unfortunately slightly indisposed.'

Lady Imogen sniffed scornfully. 'Indisposed, you say?' she said stiffly. 'Come on, Inspector, let's call a spade a spade! You know that Reverend and Mrs. Valentine, and many others' (she glanced haughtily around the company) 'have terrible hangovers!'

Sir John put a warning hand on his wife's arm. 'Hush, my dear, don't excite yourself! Although, undoubtedly, yesterday's party did get a little out of hand.'

Lady Imogen could not be silenced. 'Out of hand, you call it, John? It's more than out of hand when all one's dearest friends – one's oldest, most respectable friends – are lying around together giggling uncontrollably and behaving quite outrageously! Like lunatics with no morals at all! And then, a man is fished out of a lake, drowned, and a harmless old lady lies dead in her own bed!' She fanned herself with her hand.

The Inspector looked hard at Lady Imogen and spoke firmly. 'Please, everybody, may we do things properly, all in good order. As you know, our team of detectives have spent the morning questioning everyone involved.' He paused a moment before adding 'Well, all those who were capable of being questioned, let's say, so soon after the events. We have taken individual statements from everyone who was in this building overnight – with the exception of poor Miss Hamilton-Tracy, naturally. Now it's time to share recollections of yesterday please.'

At this point, everyone started talking at once. The Inspector raised his hand to quell the hubbub of voices.

'Thank you, ladies and gentlemen. To continue…. as you may observe, Constable Black is here to record all that is said. So we must each take our turn. First, to establish yesterday's events, in order…'

Here he was interrupted by an indignant Maude. 'But we don't even know why we're here! At least, Celia my niece, and her husband Colonel Blunkett, and I….. we only got out of bed twenty minutes ago! Who was drowned in the lake, and what's it got to do with us?'

Here Amelia burst into loud sobs, hiding her face in a sodden hanky. 'Oh, my poor dear Basil!'

Phoebe looked over at Maude's puzzled face. 'Didn't you know, Maude? The village has been buzzing, that kind of news soon gets about. But then, if you will stay in bed for hours and hours while the sun's shining…'

Maude interrupted noisily. 'Phoebe, you know very well that normally I'm up with the lark, fresh as a daisy, careering about the countryside with my little Dotty! But this morning – well, I felt a little under the weather and my eyes seemed to be glued shut against the light…'

Lady Imogen broke in sternly. 'This morning, Miss Maude Westonbury, you had a severe hangover! Very severe, I hope. Disgraceful!'

Sir John spoke up. 'Actually, Inspector, I do feel that some of those present are not likely to be very accurate witnesses.' He paused to cough behind his hand before continuing. 'I have to say, naming no names, that from my observations, many of the company were not in a fit state to know, let alone remember, what went on in this house yesterday!'

The Inspector nodded in agreement. 'Quite, Sir. Doctor Jones, whose wife' (he glanced at Phoebe) 'was a guest here yesterday, has already suggested that we should investigate the nature of the drinks served during the so-called cocktail party. That's under way. Doctor Jones is at present working with our police pathologist to establish exact causes of these unfortunate deaths. Also, from other quarters' (he gestured towards Svetla and Ivan) 'I have received information that may link these deaths to the recent sad demise of two elderly ladies in the district.'

The names 'Gladys and Elfrida', 'those poor old Pentelow sisters' were murmured around the room; heads were shaken and frowning looks were exchanged.

The Inspector waited for silence, then continued. 'So, we are also investigating what foods were consumed at the party last night.'

Amelia's sobs grew louder and took on a hysterical tone. The Inspector raised his voice a little. 'Maybe I should explain what we know already.'

Amelia stood up shakily and appealed to the Inspector. 'Please, Inspector, must I sit through this? I've just lost my Basil, and dear Aunt Hepzibah, and I feel I simply cannot endure much more.'

The Inspector regarded her, and responded with some sympathy. 'I'm sorry, Madam, but we've reached the stage when we all need to jog our memories, together, and recall yesterday's events. Do please sit down so we may continue.'

Here Mabel, usually so tongue-tied in company, butted in indignantly. 'Jog our mem'ries! That's as maybe. But there's some things as I won't ferget, not until me dyin' day!' She fixed the Colonel with an accusing stare, which seemed to mystify him. He rubbed his head as if struggling to remember, then responded slowly.

'Funny…. yesterday's events are rather vague in my memory….. just a pleasant blur, really. But I have the impression that some saucy bit of fluff was all over me. Nothing like a flighty filly to make a chap feel young again!'

Celia looked puzzled. 'A flighty filly, did you say, Mortimer? My memory's a bit foggy too, but I really don't recall any contact with horses at all!'

Her husband gave her a playful slap on the knee. 'You get my drift, old gal, I'm sure! And you yourself were unusually…. er…. animated, when we returned home. We should have more parties, it livens us all up!' He took his favourite pipe from his pocket, filled and lit it, and settled down contentedly.

Celia frowned at him. 'Mortimer, do please remember where we are and that we're here to help the police. Behave yourself!'

Her husband looked aggrieved. 'Well, it's not really my fault I'm so attractive to the ladies. It's always been the same. They just can't keep their hands off me!'

Mabel burst in again. 'It weren't my hands what were the problem, Colonel, if you recall!'

Ruby joined in. 'And I'll never be able to look the vicar in the face again. Spec'lly of a Sunday when he's spoutin' in the pulpit!'

Mary Anne was next. 'An' I'll allus be wond'rin' if Cook's goin' ter leap up any minute wivout warnin', an' go into a song-an'-dance routine!'

Once again the room was filled with mutterings, murmurings, and hot denials, until the exasperated Inspector stood up to regain order. 'Please, ladies and gentlemen! And may we have no smoking during this investigation, Colonel Blunkett, if you please!'

Looking contrite, the Colonel extinguished his pipe. The Inspector turned to the busily scribbling Constable. 'There's no need to record all that, thank you, Constable.'

When all was quiet and every face was turned towards him, the Inspector continued. 'Well, to put you all in the picture. Mr. Milanov here, and his wife, happened to hear a commotion down by the lake, late last evening, and on investigating…'

Amelia butted in angrily. 'You mean, spying!'

Ivan turned to face Amelia. 'Madam, it is part of our job to keep eye out for intruders in grounds. And we could not avoid hearing very violent argument out there.'

'And what time was this, Mr. Milanov?' enquired the Inspector.

'Just after ten o'clock, Sir, down by lake,' answered Ivan. 'My wife and I just walked down to see who it might be.'

'And did you recognise the persons?' asked the Inspector.

Svetla answered. 'Oh yes, Inspector, we knew voices all right. Madam Amelia and Mr. Charles. He sounded bit drunk. We've known them over thirty years, they were often here as children. They were very angry.' Everyone looked enquiringly at Charles (who looked both angry and confused) and at the sobbing Amelia.

The Inspector asked the Milanovs 'Could you hear what was said at all?'

'Just few odd words,' said Svetla. 'Divorce was mentioned, I know.'

Ivan spoke slowly, trying to remember exactly. 'I heard Mr. Charles say "you never could be trusted, Amelia." Well, we felt embarrassed, like we were eavesdropping.'

Amelia leaped up angrily to shout 'Which you were!'

Ignoring her outburst, Ivan continued. 'So we went back to stables. But we left window open in case of more trouble.'

Svetla joined in again. 'Then it all went quiet. But we thought we heard footsteps going up to house.'

Amelia's sobs had ceased. She now looked defiant. 'It was chilly outside. I went inside to find my warm shawl. That's not a crime, is it?'

'Certainly not, Madam,' said the Inspector soothingly. 'But let Mr. and Mrs. Milanov continue please. I've talked with them individually, of course, but now I would like everyone to know what these two saw and heard last night. It might jog a few memories.' He nodded towards the Milanovs. 'Please continue.'

'Well, next it sounded like someone going down steps, from house down to where bench is – bench by lake, where Mr. Charles and Madam Amelia had been sitting. Then, there was nothing.'

Svetla corrected her husband. 'Well…. nothing except rather strange noise….. purring noise. Ivan crept down to see what it was.'

Ivan continued. 'I saw bulky shape, like rather large person, lying full length on bench above lake. Snoring, very loud. It was dark, cloudy, no moon. I couldn't be sure who it was. But everything was calm, he wasn't causing trouble. So I went back to stable block.'

Svetla took over. 'We went to bed after that. We left window open. Then I thought I heard something, but no voices. I looked out and couldn't see anything. I was tired, I went to sleep.'

Ivan said 'I stayed awake. I couldn't sleep at first. Then I heard loud splash. I got out of bed but there was no more sound, nothing moving. I thought it was animals, or leaping fish. There are big pike in lake, you know. In few minutes, I dozed off.'

Svetla said 'We woke up late this morning. We had busy week, getting ready for party, tidying garden.'

Everyone had been listening with bated breath to the Milanov's story. Charles would not meet anyone's eye, keeping his head down. Amelia once again buried her face in her hanky, her shoulders shaking with sobs.

'You have been most helpful, thank you,' said the Inspector to the Milanovs. 'Now, to explain today's events. This morning we had a call at Headquarters from Mr. Charles Hamilton-Tracy. He told us he had seen a large clothed human body lying in the lake here, near the bank, in shallow water. Only the head and shoulders were submerged. The rest of the body lay in soft mud.'

Amelia began to shriek hysterically at these words. Phoebe went over to her and put an arm around her shaking shoulders. Charles confirmed the Inspector's account. 'That's right. My fiancée Candida and I went for an early morning walk. It was a beautiful morning and we had a lot to talk about. And I needed to clear my head somehow, I had a terrible headache.'

Candida, at Charles's side, spoke for the first time, her voice tremulous. 'It was a dreadful shock, I'll never forget that moment. Horrible! I had never met Mr. Bantam-Cox until yesterday, at the party. And I've never seen a dead person before.' Charles put a protective arm around her and leaned close.

The Inspector addressed Charles. 'Thank you for contacting us so promptly, Sir. Of course, our men went down and checked the area for footprints, any clue as to how or why the gentleman came to be lying in the lake. The water's really quite shallow. An injured man, for instance a man who'd received a blow on the head and who was stunned, might have conceivably drowned in such shallow water. But any reasonably fit person would have been able to scramble out. There were no marks of injury on Mr. Bantam-Cox at all.'

Now there were voices outside the room. Everyone looked over to see who was coming, and saw Reverend Bertram Valentine and Dorothy his wife being ushered in by a police Officer. The Vicar looked around, rather shamefaced, at his parishioners.

'Do please forgive us, everybody, for our tardiness. My wife and I slept rather late this morning. I do beg your pardon,' he said politely.

At his side, Dorothy looked around in bewilderment at all the faces turned towards her, saying 'I do hope nothing untoward has occurred. Seeing police all over the village is really rather disturbing, you know.'

The Inspector gave a slight bow towards the newcomers. 'Do sit down, dear lady. And you too, Vicar. I'm sorry to tell you we are gathered here because of a tragedy. We are trying to establish just why and how Mr. Basil Bantam-Cox came to drown in very shallow water, some time in the night.'

Dorothy, who had just sat wearily down, leaped up in horror. 'Mr. Bantam-Cox is drowned! Why, we only met him yesterday! How dreadful!'

Lady Imogen looked coolly over at Dorothy, saying haughtily 'If I recall correctly, Dorothy, a variety of rather dreadful things occurred yesterday.' She looked disapprovingly at Reverend Valentine, and added 'Isn't that so, Reverend?'

The Reverend looked nonplussed. 'Really, Lady Imogen? I don't recall anything untoward. Just a fine party. I must say, our walk home seemed rather arduous. But once we got safely to bed, we slept well, unusually well.'

Sir John regarded his friend Bertram sternly. 'It appears to me that the well-known phrase "the dignity of the cloth" rings a bit hollow today…. wouldn't you agree, Bertram?'

The Reverend replied huffily. 'I really don't know what you mean, Sir John. I must say I felt the party was rather jolly.'

Dorothy looked fondly at her bewildered husband. 'I think we should have more parties, dear. You were in a very good mood last night.... very charming, very affectionate!'

Ruby could not contain herself. She jumped up and confronted the Vicar. 'I din't think you was charmin', Vicar. In fact I dun't want to work at the Vicarage no more!'

'Why, what do you mean, Ruby?' enquired the mystified Bertram. 'You and I have always got on so well and you do a fine job for Dorothy and myself.'

'I'm sorry, but I wun't feel comf'table at the Vic'rage after yest'd'y!' said Ruby.

'Oh, Ruby, that is most distressing!' said Dorothy sorrowfully. 'Please don't leave us.' Ruby continued to glare hotly but was slightly mollified by these kind words.

The Inspector sighed wearily. 'Maybe you could discuss this later, Reverend and Mrs. Valentine? We have very important matters to attend to here.'

The Vicar nodded and led his wife to the two chairs Sir John had brought forward for his friends. Sir John couldn't be angry with Bertram for long; he was such a pleasant, self-effacing chap.

Maude now called out loudly. 'That was the best party I've been to for years! Rotten about Mr. Bantam-Cox, though. Maybe he just tripped in the dark. Maybe he was drunk!'

Candida spoke again. 'But.... he was in the kitchen, with me and the maid. He was eating party food and talking quite sensibly, late in the evening. He seemed perfectly clear-headed – although he told us he had fallen asleep earlier. I know he wasn't carrying a bottle, or even a glass, because he was holding a plate and eating vol-au-vents. Then he suddenly said he needed some fresh air. Said he'd just walk down to the lake to find his wife.'

Mary Anne confirmed this. 'That's right. I were tidyin' up. I were right there!'

The Inspector asked 'Was anyone else in the kitchen at the time, Miss?'

'Cook were there, but she were fast asleep, snorin'!' announced Mary Anne.

Cook, who had seemed half asleep and who had been yawning all afternoon, now leaped up indignantly. 'I'll thank you not to tell such wicked untruths about me, Mary Anne! I dun't sleep on duty! I earns me keep!'

Mary Anne held her ground. 'Sorry, Cook. I knows you'm a right good worker, and I've never seed you like that afore. But you was snorin' right loud! Then Mr. Charles come in an' started talkin' with 'er,' she indicated Candida. 'I dun't know 'er name.'

Charles took over the tale. 'Then Cook suddenly woke up and started leaping around! Quite an amazing sight, I couldn't believe my eyes! And she started singing, and trying to get me to dance with her!'

'That's right,' put in Candida. 'It was quite extraordinary!'

Cook's mouth was hanging open. A look of disbelief was on her kindly old face. 'I dun't dance 'n sing! With my legs, it's a wonder I can even walk!' A thoughtful, puzzled look crossed her ruddy features. 'But, it's funny.... 'cos when I woke up this mornin', me whole body were achin'. Mebbe I really were dancin' yesterd'y!'

The Inspector addressed Cook. 'Well, as there was a party in progress, did you by any chance partake of a drink or two with the guests, Cook? Speak up if you did. It would be quite understandable, nobody would blame you.'

Cook hotly denied this possibility. 'But... I'm teetotal! I'm Chapel, you know. We all foreswears strong drink at Chapel! I never touches a drop. But.... it were a reely strange evenin', summat funny were goin' on. I reely 'ave no mem'ry of yesterd'y evenin' at all. Nothin' after about six o'clock, me 'ead's a blank. But I do feel bad that I din't go into Miss 'amilton-Tracy's room to check she were all right.'

Mary Anne spoke up. 'I 'ad a reel bad shock when I went in with 'er toast an' tea this mornin' an' found 'er there so dead an' all!'

Dorothy looked up, shocked. 'Miss Hepzibah dead! No-one told us. How sad, just after her birthday. Maybe the celebration tired her.'

Reverend Valentine commented, 'Since the dear lady stayed in her bed throughout the evening, and we only disturbed her by singing to her, I feel that was rather a pleasant last day. But we had no idea she had passed away. How sad!'

Lady Imogen addressed the Vicar in sarcastic tones. 'Oh, you call that singing, do you, Bertram? For myself, I thought it the most appalling caterwauling. Just like a crowd of drunken sailors!'

'Drunken sailors?' interjected Mary Anne. 'That's funny. Cook were singin' about drunken sailors last night!'

'Watch yer mouth, gel!' said Cook. 'I've 'ad enough o' this. Mebbe me mem'ry went 'cos I'd worked so darn hard all week. But.... I do 'ave a feelin' of enjoyin' that party, even if I can't remember it.'

'Cook, do you remember eating any of the party food?' asked the Inspector. 'Even if you had none of the drink?'

'Well – I did 'ave the odd tidbit,' mused Cook. 'I 'ad to check ev'rythin' I made were up to standard, y'see. I was kep' too busy to 'ave time fer eatin', reely. Run off me feet! But... I do remember scrapin' out a bowl, some fish an' mushroom mixture Miss Amelia – that is, Mrs. Bantam-Cox – prepared fer the last o' them vollavong cases. I scraped out the bowl before I washed it, y'see.'

Amelia was heard to gasp. Heads turned towards her. She was sitting in forlorn desolation, her head in her hands.

The Constable looked up in exasperation. ''Ere, 'old yer 'orses! How do you spell that vollavong thing every one keeps going on about?'

The Inspector responded calmly. 'Just write V-V, Constable, and we'll sort it out back at the station.' He turned to Mary Anne. 'Did you by chance eat any of that mixture, Miss?'

'No Sir', replied Mary Anne. 'I were too busy.... 'spec'lly after Cook went to sleep and the other gels run off 'ome, and all the work were left ter me.'

'And how was that mixture used, for the party food, please?'

'Well,' said Mary Anne, 'Mrs. Bantam-Cox..... Madam Amelia, that is...... she filled the last vollavong pastry cases with it. They was the ones Mr. Basil was eatin'. Said he found 'em on top of the tall chest in poor Miss 'epzibah's room. He ate the last three.'

'Did he, indeed?' responded the Inspector thoughtfully.

Amelia was seen to be sobbing loudly once more, and although muffled by the handkerchief she clutched to her tearful face, the words 'Oh, my poor dear silly Basil!' were heard.

The Reverend now spoke up. 'But tell us, Inspector, how did poor Miss Hamilton-Tracy pass away?'

Phoebe turned towards the Vicar. 'You know, Vicar, my husband has been her doctor for years. Walter always said she might pass on any day. Ninety's a good age.'

'Very true, very true,' said the Inspector. 'At first it seemed likely that the old lady simply slipped peacefully away. But now, we're wondering...... maybe someone helped her on her way, so to speak.' He addressed Mary Anne. 'Now, Miss. You say Mr. Bantam-Cox found the vol-au-vents he consumed in Miss Hamilton-Tracy's room. Did you take them in there?'

'No, she'd not touch rich food like them anymore, Sir. We jus' give 'er tea an' toast an' a little beef broth, like on other days.'

The Inspector raised an enquiring eyebrow. 'So.... who took the vol-au-vents into her room and left them there, do you think, Miss?'

'Well, I remember Madam Amelia took that plate into the drawing room first,' said Mary Anne. 'Then she did say she were goin' into Miss 'epzibah's room, to see 'ow she were doin'. I dun't know if she took that plate in wiv 'er, I were busy in the kitchen.' Amelia's sobs grew to a crescendo and many of the listeners took a surreptitious peep at her. Phoebe patted her warmly on the shoulder.

'I see. Thank you,' said the Inspector. He turned to Cook. 'And can you tell me, Cook, who concocted the fruit punch that was given to the guests?'

'Oh, that were Madam Amelia,' answered Cook with confidence. 'I were right surprised she wanted to do it. First time she ever took an interest in what goes on in my kitchen!'

Amelia sat up, and raised her tear-streaked face. With an effort, she swallowed hard and forced herself to speak. 'That was something I learned out in Kenya….. how to make a party go with a swing! I really wanted a good send-off …. er….. I mean, celebration…… for dear Auntie, you see. I really loved poor Auntie!'

Under her breath, Cook was heard to murmur 'Loved 'er money, she means!'

'Quite so. I'm afraid some unusual and illegal substances seem to have got into those jugs,' commented the Inspector, continuing with a note of sarcasm in his voice. 'Something else you learned in Kenya, I suppose?'

Amelia kept her head down and didn't attempt an answer.

Sir John turned apologetically towards Reverend Valentine. 'I feel this somewhat explains your…. er…. eccentric behaviour yesterday, dear Bertram. I must confess that my wife and I were considerably shocked when we came upon the party scene yesterday. You and the Colonel were…. er ….. behaving with some impropriety, I'm afraid. Dorothy and Celia were squabbling like children, and Mr. Charles and poor Mr. Bantam-Cox were fighting on the floor!'

Shock and embarrassment were visible in the Vicar's expression as he turned to look around the company, saying in contrite tones 'Is that so? I do apologise!'

Friendly murmurs arose all over the room. 'That's all right, Bertram!' 'Not your fault I'm sure, Vicar!' and so on.

Sir John continued. 'I'm afraid the effects were quite long lasting. Imogen and I, of course, did what we could to help. We were able to take Phoebe, and dear Dorothy who unfortunately was in no fit state to walk, to their homes, in the Wolseley. But you and the Colonel, and Celia and Maude, set off to walk.'

The accusing voice of Lady Imogen continued the tale. 'It wasn't really walking, as I recall! More like a wild three-legged race in the Infants' Class!'

'And when last seen…. and heard….. there was a rabble, including you, Bertram' (here Sir John looked severely at the hapless Vicar) 'rolling around singing and giggling in the front gardens of the Drift Cottages. I've heard the Brown family were quite taken aback!'

The Vicar was now pink in the face and didn't know where to look. 'Dear dear, how very regrettable… I am so sorry!' he murmured. Apologies were offered from others in the room. No-one doubted Sir John's word. Dorothy, blushing profusely, took her husband's hand, as his partner in crime.

Lady Imogen could not let the matter drop. 'A truly shocking example to the lower classes! Quite mortifying!'

Her husband whispered in her ear, persuading her that the matter was over and done with and now best forgotten.

The Inspector had listened with great interest to these exchanges. 'Thank you everybody, maybe we can consign these incidents to the past now. You may like to know that, given the nature of the substances found in the jugs used for fruit punch, such behaviour was only to be expected. No blame attaches to these unfortunate guests. No blame at all! It seems some person wanted to ensure that no-one was quite in charge of their senses at the cocktail party......' He paused and wrote something on his copious pile of notes, before continuing, 'presumably to make sure that they were unable to accurately observe what was going on.'

A cloud seemed to lift from those accused of shameful behaviour, and they began to hold their heads high and bravely meet the eyes of their neighbours. Lady Imogen was on her feet again, imperiously demanding the attention of the Inspector. 'I was in charge of my senses, Inspector. And I remember something very strange was happening when John and I entered the room. Amelia was trying to get Charles to eat some food. He was on the floor, and she was practically on her knees beside him, trying to feed him like a baby!'

'Yes, it was disgusting!' growled Charles. 'Can't stand fishy things....I spat them out!'

Amelia called out wildy. 'You spat them out? So that's why.....' her voice trailed into silence.

'Then,' said Lady Imogen, fixing Amelia with a steely stare, 'when her husband.... poor Mr. Bantam-Cox..... tried to help himself from the plate, she wouldn't let him!'

Sir John spoke thoughtfully. 'Yes, my dear, I too noticed that she snatched the plate out of his reach and hurried out of the room. Very strange behaviour for a hostess.'

Amelia was standing up, swaying slightly. She had gone very pale. She began to move towards the door. 'I'm sorry, but I must go to my room and lie down for a while. Don't forget I've just been widowed, I've lost my dear Basil!'

Charles leaped up and barred her way, shouting. 'No, you haven't! I mean, yes, you have lost Basil. That's terrible and we're all very sorry for you. But you haven't been widowed! I'm still your husband, Amelia!'

At these words Amelia sank down again, wailing miserably. Candida now sprang from her chair and grabbed Charles by the arm, screaming almost as loudly as Amelia.

'But Charles! You're engaged to me!' The room fell suddenly silent. Then everybody seemed to draw breath at the same time. Charles was looking uncomfortable. He said desperately 'Yes, darling. I am so sorry! I mean, I'm not sorry I'm engaged to you, of course. I'm sorry I haven't been quite straight with you. That's why I came down to Wood Hall. It's why I returned to England in the first place. Someone told me Amelia was married to a Mr. Bantam-Cox. I said nothing, but inside I was furious, because Amelia has been married to me for nearly nine years!'

Candida's face was a picture of grief and bewilderment. She sat down again, staring at Charles in shock, as if she could not believe he had said these dreadful words.

Maude called out loudly. 'Amelia married to Charles! Why were we not told? Where was the wedding?'

Amelia now spoke in a subdued, hopeless voice, not looking at anyone, her head bowed low. 'In Kenya. We were married in Kenya. I was out there working as a governess. I hated being with those squabbling whipper-snappers all day, and I was lonely. Charles was working on the tea plantation my employers owned. I had only gone out there to be near Charles. And he proposed to me.'

Celia was curious. 'But why was your marriage a secret?'

'Because I didn't want Auntie to know. We were miles from England and we kept the wedding very quiet. You see, Charles and I were always together on our holidays here with Auntie. I remember, when I was about seven, and Charles must have been about nine, Auntie asked me what I wanted to do when I grew up. Of course, I said "I'll marry Charles!" He was my hero, you see.' She paused, looking miserably downcast, then continued. 'But Auntie said "One thing you should know, Amelia. Cousins should never marry. It's a very unlucky thing to do, so let's hear no more about marrying Charles." Auntie was really quite scary when she was annoyed. So I never forgot that day. I didn't want her to know, I didn't want to upset her.'

Charles scowled at her. 'You mean, you didn't want her to cut you out of her will!'

Amelia's face became red with anger. 'Don't say that, Charles! I loved Auntie, not her money!'

The Inspector spoke. 'May I ask what led to your separation, Sir?'

Charles hesitated at first, then explained. 'Well, like her Father, Amelia had a taste for parties and strong drink. She really got quite wild in the Kenyan high-life that went on. That was bad for my reputation and my work prospects. She let me down publicly, time and time again….'

Amelia screeched at him. 'Charles! I only wanted a good time! Besides, I was bored. And the parties were fun!'

Charles scowled at her. 'Do you remember, Amelia, that dinner with my Boss, where you fell asleep in the dessert? You had been drinking non-stop. At the party you behaved in a most promiscuous manner. I didn't know where to look! Then in the middle of the meal, your head flopped forward into the trifle and you started snoring!'

Amelia pouted crossly. 'Shut up, Charles! That was years and years ago!' Whispering was heard among the listeners, and people craned their necks to see the warring couple better. Heads were shaken, expressions became self-righteous.

Charles took up the story again. He glared at the cringing Amelia. 'I was humiliated by your behaviour, Amelia. Totally humiliated. I had to half carry you out of that dinner party – with my Boss watching me – and my new dinner jacket got covered with whipped cream and strawberry mousse!'

'I was young, I wasn't used to strong drink!' wailed Amelia.

'Not used to strong drink?' said Charles scornfully. 'You were certainly intent on getting used to it! You drank from morning till night. Cost me a fortune, and nearly cost me my job.' He turned to address the Inspector. 'So you see, Inspector, I told Amelia to go home to England, grow up and sober up, until she was ready to be a proper wife. And I never saw her again until yesterday!'

'It's all your fault, Charles!' wailed Amelia. 'You ruined everything for me!'

'Dash it all, Amelia!' said Charles. 'you were just a dead weight, pulling me down! All the servants and tea-pickers used to snigger behind their backs when they saw me. How could I maintain any air of authority? And I think my boss was thinking, how can a man control scores of natives if he can't even control his own wife?'

'You were so hard on me, Charles. Not loving, at all. When I married you, I thought it would be fun, like when we were children. But all you ever did was find fault with me. I was happy with my Basil, he enjoyed life, like me. He didn't know I'd been married before. He thought my name was still Amelia Fleetwood when he married me. We had a lovely life at first. Only, his Father had a rough time on the Stock Market, then his family home was re-possessed by the Bank, just like mine. Basil and I had nowhere to go, except to Wood Hall, here with Auntie. And now I've got nobody!' Amelia burst into loud sobs. Phoebe, who had been visibly shocked by all these revelations, continued to comfort her as best she could.

Charles had not finished yet. 'Sorry if I've been hard on you, sweet cousin. But, when you came back here, I reckon you were thinking, the old girl will soon be dead and she'll leave everything to me!'

Amelia managed to quell her tears for long enough to say defiantly 'No, I didn't! Actually I thought she'd leave half to me and half to you. We're her

only relatives now. But when you arrived here yesterday, I thought you might tell Aunt how we got married in Kenya. I had told her Basil was my husband. So then she would know I had committed bigamy, and be angry, and cut me out of her Will, and you'd get everything. Then I thought, Charles will be angry because I married Basil, and Basil will get jealous when he hears I was married to you, Charles. And then Basil might leave me. And then, I'd be all alone in the world with no-one loving me, not a penny to my name, and nowhere to live! I suppose I got in a panic really.'

The Inspector was regarding Amelia steadily. 'Seems we're hearing something of the truth at last, Madam. Thank you. That's always best in the end, you know.'

Amelia started to sob again. 'I loved my Basil, I really loved him. He was kinder to me than you ever were, Charles. He never criticised me. The only problem was we had no money and no home!'

Svetla began to speak, her face eager. 'Now I understand! When I saw you, Amelia, rushing through park with basket yesterday, then sneaking back into Wood Hall by servants' entrance, I was mystified. Now I know what was in that basket. It was Fly Agaric mushrooms from other side of woods near Gladys and Elfrida's cottage!'

Amelia had gone scarlet. Her eyes widened in fear as others spoke up against her.

'I saw you near that cottage,' said Maude, 'under the trees, filling your basket. You were so busy searching among the leaves that you didn't notice me. I'd just gone to have another look at the cottage, with my Dotty, thinking about those two old hags and what happened to them there.'

Cook spoke next. 'So that's what you was a–mixin' up in me kitchen, Miss! I remember you was busy with me bowls, me spoons, an' some o' me delicious sauce, standin' wiv yer back to me, hidin' summat. But I was run orf me feet so I just got on, cooking me brandy snaps an' me devilled eggs!'

Amelia raised her swollen, tear-stained face. She was overwhelmed with emotion and close to hysteria. Her audience hung on her every word, straining to hear through her sobs. 'I never meant to hurt my Basil! It was you, Charles! I just wanted you to disappear, back to Kenya for ever. I wanted to persuade you to keep quiet about our marriage and just go back to the plantation. I thought there might be a way you could get us divorce papers in Kenya – without telling them over there that I had already married again. I was desperate for you to go away without Auntie finding out what I'd done. I'd told her I was married to Basil. She would have thought bigamy was even more shameful than marrying a cousin! And I was hurt and angry and scared yesterday, when you arrived here out of the blue and told me that you wanted a divorce and you had a new fiancée. Stuck up Madam!' She glared at Candida, who was now looking less desperate and was hanging on to Charles's arm.

'You're jealous because Charles wants me now, not you, you minx! He's mine! He loves me, and I love him! And I've been so terribly lonely since I lost my Cuthbert, my first husband!' Candida mopped her eyes with a small white hanky.

Charles leaned close to her, saying 'Candida darling, we will get married, don't be scared!' He then looked at Amelia coldly. 'So, Amelia, I suppose that when we sat on that bench near the edge of the lake last night – when you said you wanted to talk to me, and led me into the garden and down to the lake – you were waiting hopefully for me to collapse into a deep sleep so you could shove me in the water and see the back of me!'

Fear showed in Amelia's dark eyes. 'No! No, Charles, how can you think that of me? I would never do a thing like that! You were my hero when we were children.'

Charles was not convinced. 'Don't try to fool me, Amelia, I know you too well. Your clever plan went wrong, didn't it? I'll tell you why. When you went back indoors for your shawl, I sat there on the bench, with my head spinning. It was getting dark as well as cold. I was feeling really odd, sort of out of my head. Now I realise that was from drinking your devilish fruit punch. Lord knows what was in it! I was furious with you about the muddle we were in, with you going through a so-called marriage when you were still married to me. I was wishing I had told Candida my real situation. I love her and I want to be honest with her. I was thinking, Candida will never trust me again when she finds out I'm already married. What a mess!'

'Poor Charles!' murmured Candida, 'no wonder you were upset!'

Charles kissed her lightly on the cheek before continuing. 'I thought maybe a little walk would calm me down, and clear my head. So I walked around the lake and through the flower garden. Then I went indoors to find my poor fiancée.'

The Inspector joined in, saying 'I think I'm right in saying that this was about the time when Mr. Bantam-Cox was finishing those last vol-au-vents, and wondering where on earth his wife had got to, and why she was out in the garden, in the dark, with her handsome cousin. So naturally he set off to find her. Having consumed those last vol-au-vents, which contained dangerous fungi, he found the empty bench by the lake most inviting. The fungus caused him to fall into a deep sleep, which was soon drastically curtailed when Madam Amelia returned, heard the snores, imagined the comatose figure was Charles, and shoved him in the lake!'

Amelia blanched. 'No, Inspector!' she screamed. 'I just wanted Charles to go back to Kenya and get a divorce over there! I was trying to persuade him that would be best!'

'In that case, Madam, what was the point of doping the other guests with spiked punch, and trying very hard to make your cousin Charles eat poisonous fungi? Unless, of course, you had a double motive, and intended to feed the fungus mix to your elderly Aunt, so she would pass away before finding out about your two so-called marriages, and not have any reason to change her Will!'

Amelia looked terrified. 'Why are you saying such terrible things about me? It's not fair! I won't say another word until someone finds me a good solicitor. You can't keep me here anyway, I'm leaving!' So saying she made for the door.

'Not so fast, Madam!' said the Inspector, as Constable Black, glad to play an active role in the drama, ran to bar her way and led her firmly back to her chair. Amelia subsided. After all, how could she escape from this mansion, surrounded by parkland and woods, without a key to any of the cars lined up outside, and with everyone against her? She sat, pale and stony faced, her head whirling.

Amid the gasps of shock, horror, excitement and even sympathy that now filled the room, a strange gurgling sound began to be heard. Everyone looked around. Svetla and Ivan were seen to be clutching at each other and starting to laugh uncontrollably.

The Inspector gazed at them, astonished. 'Mr. and Mrs. Milanov! Surely this is no laughing matter?'

Lady Imogen arose up in her haughtiest manner, saying sternly 'Might we all behave in a more seemly fashion, please? After all, two people have died in this sordid affair.'

Svetla made a visible effort to control herself. 'I'm so sorry, Lady Imogen, I forgot myself. But you see, I just saw funny side! About two years ago, Miss Hamilton-Tracy told us she was changing her Will. There wasn't much money left anyway, she had bought so many race horses, and they never won races for her.'

'And she loved travelling!' broke in Ivan. 'She loved travelling world. Liked first-class tickets and best hotels. Always travelling. That's how she met me and wife.'

Maude said 'Yes, I remember when you two came to Meadowford. You didn't know a word of the lingo then!'

Ivan explained. 'Back in Old Bohemia I drove coach and four. Miss

Hamilton-Tracy saw I had way with horses and asked us to come to England and work in stables with race horses. That was something new and I thought, why not see more of world? So we travelled to England with her and we've been here ever since.'

Svetla spoke. 'Lady kept spending and spending. Always buying horses, saddles, and everything best quality. Two years ago she told us Wood Hall was security for Bank loan. All servants and gardeners were dismissed except us, Cook, and Mary Anne.'

Amelia shrieked. 'I don't believe you! Auntie was stinking rich, my Mother said so. Mother knew, she was Auntie's sister, but my grandparents believed Mother was a waster who couldn't be trusted, and left everything to Auntie. It wasn't fair! How will I live now, no home, no money, no friends, and my poor Basil drowned!' She buried her face in her hands.

Phoebe, who wasn't quite sure whether she should be comforting a suspected murderer, once again put an arm around those heaving shoulders. She tried to think of some comforting words, but was at a total loss in this unfamiliar situation.

The Inspector said drily to Amelia 'Don't worry, Madam. I believe you will be adequately fed, clothed and housed "At His Majesty's pleasure" for a while.'

The Vicar whispered in his wife's ear 'How cruel, we must see if we can help somehow'. Dorothy, who was horribly shocked, nodded dumbly.

Ivan continued to enlighten the unfortunate Amelia. 'I'm sorry to disappoint you, Madam Amelia, but your Aunt told us any money remaining after Hall is taken by Bank and affairs put in order, will be shared between me, my wife, Mary Anne and Cook.'

Svetla, rubbing salt into the wounds, added 'You and Mr. Charles are not down to get single penny! Sorry!'

Cook and Mary Anne were dumbfounded, and stared at each other wide-eyed.

'What, left to us? She never said nothin' to us!' said Cook eventually.

Mary Anne, shaking her head but grinning foolishly, replied 'Cor, blow me down! Glory be!'

Amelia whimpered '.... and the only thing in the world that was mine, my kind Basil, drowned in the lake! Why did the idiot have to fall asleep on that bench, just where Charles and I had been sitting?' Realising too late the stupidity of voicing her true thoughts in this sharp-eared company, she clamped her hand across her mouth.

Charles accused her once more. 'Now I understand why you thought I was a ghost when I walked into the kitchen, looking for Candida. You thought I'd snuffed it. Sorry, Amelia, but I'm still very much alive. And you've given me ample grounds for divorce, so thank you!' He honoured Amelia with a mock bow before sitting down.

This was too much for kind Bertram to watch. He spoke to the company in general, saying 'How distressing! Dangerous mix, you know, despair plus panic plus high emotions. Can impair a person's judgement!'

Lady Imogen stood up to refer once again to certain other cases of impaired judgement witnessed at the cocktail party, but her voice was thankfully drowned by Colonel Mortimer's deep growl. 'That was a ripping party, quite made me feel like a young dog again! So thanks, Amelia!'

The Inspector had gathered up his books, thanked all present for their kind co-operation, and was following Amelia (firmly held in Constable Black's strong grasp) to the door, when a hubbub broke out behind them. Cook had grabbed Mary Anne's hands and was whirling her around as fast as her plump old legs could manage, while bursting into song. 'What shall we do with the drunken sailor?' began to resound about the long room. Charles stood up and made for the drinks cabinet, crying 'What about a little drink, friends? Maybe champers, this time!'

Against the better judgement of some of the company, sombre faces broke into smiles, heads began to nod in assent, and the Vicar proposed a toast.

'I propose a toast! To tender-hearted judges, a merciful God, Miss Hamilton Tracy and Mr. Bantam-Cox – God rest their souls – and to ....er....absent friends and the future!'

All around, inhibitions were cast to the winds and glasses were raised, as the residents of Meadowford joined the chorus 'Cheers! To absent friends, and the future!'

THE END

OTHER BOOKS BY SHEILA WRIGHT
All shown on www.kisumubooks.co.uk

DRINKSTONE : SCHOOL & VILLAGE
A Suffolk History
Greenridges Press

Extract from Review in magazine 'Suffolk / Norfolk Life',
December 2009 Issue –

'This local history tells the story of one Church of England school in its
village context. Drinkstone School was built in 1861 and enlarged in 1912 but
spent many of its final years under threat of closure. It was starved of funds for
essential modernisation work (such as the installation of flush toilets), but the
dedication of its teachers and the lively spirit of its pupils ensured that it was a
stimulating and happy place in which to learn. The school finally closed in
1986 and, after standing sadly derelict, has now been converted into a
delightful house…..

A strong feature of the book is dozens of vivid personal stories and
reminiscences of ex-pupils, staff and villagers. Several contributors are now
aged over ninety. Their stories take us back in time and enable us to share
intimate details of other lives…..

The book is richly illustrated with archive photographs and plans, and also
with Sheila's own drawings. Many of the beautiful historic buildings of
Drinkstone are featured.'

ISBN 1-902019-08-5 Price 10.99 (plus P & P)

DRINKSTONE REVISITED
more stories from a Suffolk village
Kisumu Books

Extract from Review in magazine 'Suffolk / Norfolk Life',
February 2010 Issue -

'This local history came about as a result of the enthusiastic response from readers of Sheila Wright's first book of Drinkstone history. The stories provide an enchanting, nostalgic and often awe-inspiring insight into country lives during recent centuries. Every facet of life is represented – life in war and peace, joy or sorrow, sickness or health, of destitute cottagers, hard-working labourers and domestics, priests, professional or tradespeople – even of landed gentry and 'noblemen'.

Sincere thanks are due to the many folk who lent treasured family photographs for inclusion in this history. The stories are put into context of time and place through the inclusion of historic maps, and a demographic overview of the village in the 19th century.

The book includes studies of several historic cottages, farmhouses, and imposing country houses in the parish. Owners and past owners of these generously offered maps, plans, photographs and knowledge.'

ISBN 9-780955-541704 Price £10.99 (plus p & p)

Extract from Review of the two Drinkstone Histories, by Doona Turner –

'Both books are a mix of researched history from Archive and other documents, interspersed with personal memories of residents, ex-residents, and their descendants.
These personal memories give life to the books and open a window on country lives and education through the decades. As far as possible people's stories are told in their own words and they make lively reading, sometimes comic, sometimes heart-breaking. I cannot emphasise enough the fascinating reading that these books make for people who enjoy local history and a bit of nostalgia.'

One of dozens of letters from ex-pupils of Drinkstone School –
'Thank you very much for the wonderful Drinkstone books. It was 68 years ago that I lived and went to school in Drinkstone but the books made it seem like last week. Thank you for the work you've done to bring lots of us such great and happy memories'.

Gordon Maile, UK (admitted as a pupil in 1944)

COMING THROUGH – THE LONG JOURNEY
The story of Ruth Elizabeth Jane Minns and Henry Moyse Gobbit (married in Bredfield, Suffolk, 1898) and their families. Archive research by David P. Gobbitt.
Kisumu Books

This is an unusual book, motivated by strange events that occurred in the village of Drinkstone, central Suffolk, over many years. While being the story of certain families and particular people in those families, in a broader sense it explores the long journey of life, through 'birth', 'death' and beyond.

Readers may come to understand a little more fully how the way we each live our lives affects others; how we live in and through each other, not just in our own small circle but throughout the generations of linked souls.

Comments from readers –

'Finally picked up the book I bought from you and found it thoroughly engrossing, couldn't put it down! Not just another family history book. The story was compelling and so well written....'

Neil Langridge, historian and author, UK

'Thanks so much for sending me my copy of your book. I was very pleased with the way you handled sensitive issues but were very fair and didn't hold back on truth! I'm sure it will help many family members answer that question of 'why are we the way we are?' and help us in our journey...

Ruth Gobbitt, Mudgee, Australia

'I've just surfaced from your book having spent three hours reading it after only intending to skim it and read it later. What a treasure! I'm so moved that you've spent so much time, energy and love uncovering and telling the story of my ancestors. I'm especially grateful for the little quotes from R.E.J. herself, at the tops of the last chapters...'

Paul Newman, UK

'My colleague Patricia Fluckiger-Livingstone said that she literally couldn't put the book down, and read it at a single sitting!'

'Mary Whyman has asked me to convey her thanks to you. She was captivated from the first page....'

ISBN 978-0-9555417-7-3 Price £12.99 (plus p & p)

BON COURAGE, MES AMIS!
Thoughts on restoring a rural ruin
Leonie Press

This book (written in English despite the title!) tells the story of the excitement of finding, purchasing and then renovating an ancient building in central France. The author received a gift of money, sufficient only to purchase something at the very bottom end of the market. She fell foolishly in love with a granite-built fermette (farm buildings and living room all under one roof). The stables at one end still housed horses in the 1960s, but no-one had used the living quarters since the 1940s and many walls were crumbling and cracked.

The features that captured Sheila Wright's romantic heart were the outside stone staircase leading to the first floor, and the location – in a small friendly hamlet, surrounded by its own garden and with views over valleys, gentle hills and woodlands.

For almost twenty years, Sheila and her long-suffering husband Ron have travelled over to this rustic retreat two or three times a year, striving to create a holiday home which is weatherproof and sound and has basic modern facilities. Despite mistakes and unwise decisions (and despite Sheila's basic ignorance of building techniques and traditional local vernacular), those years have been full of fun and achievement. Getting to know the neighbours, creating a garden, entertaining friends and family, observing a rural life-style which has survived over centuries and is gradually disappearing as the modern world encroaches – the memories are unforgettable.

A Reader in New Zealand wrote to say –'From the very beginning of your book I wanted to write to you....I love France and have read a good many books similar to yours, though seldom as good and genuine, from the heart.....congratulations on your excellent taste and the honesty of your writing...'

Hugh Oliver, New Zealand

ISBN 1-901253-30-9 £8.99 (plus p & p)

A ZEST FOR LIFE
Biography of economist David B. Jones told in letters
Kisumu Books

David Jones was a man who made the most of life. His fifty-four years were packed full of enterprise and adventure. These letters tell the story of David and his family, his years at Oxford University, his enthusiasms, his concern over world politics, third-world development and agriculture, and his special love for Africa.

The letters recount experiences in Europe, the USA, the West Indies, India, Bhutan, numerous African countries and more. He was an acute observer of life and people in every location he encountered. All life was an adventure. His fund of knowledge and experience made his letters home a treasure to those who received them, meaning hundreds survived to provide this compelling record of a gifted and lovable man.

David met an untimely death in Chad. His body was flown home in the President's own plane. Despite the unexpectedness of this death and the distances involved, many people who had worked with him (mainly Africans) attended the funeral in Bedford. One huge and stunningly-attired African had a long talk with the family, explaining why David was held in such high esteem. He praised his easy approachability and down-to-earth practical attitude. For example, if the job in hand entailed vaccinating a herd of cows, David would not stand aloof, watching, like the majority of white officials. He would be right in there, helping herd the cows, getting his hands dirty, sharing the work. And he was always ready to converse with the poorest of the poor, listening to their stories as one human being to another.

Extract from a letter received from a cousin of David Jones, 26th January 2009

'Many thanks for sending me 'A Zest for Life' which arrived today. So far I have only skimmed through it briefly, but enough for me to realise what a massive task you set yourself and how well you have achieved it. I had no idea that David had done so much with his life. Congratulations on having produced such a splendid memorial to David. And I must add, you do write very well indeed…'

Herbert Jones, UK

ISBN 9-780955-541728 £14.50 (plus p & p)

GUHRETEN
A FANTASY by ALISTAIR JONES
Kisumu Books

Alistair is the eldest grandson of David Jones, and is the only one of his grandchildren whom David was able to know. Alistair was aged two when his Grandpa died. David would have been so proud of all of them if he had lived.

Alistair won a story writing competition at the age of twelve. His story is lively and engaging, illustrated by himself. Many children have bought and enjoyed this book, and in fact it has been purchased as an 'English Reader' by a school in central France. Copies have also gone to a school in Afghanistan whose pupils had nothing much except the building and some tables and chairs. An International best-seller!

ISBN 0-955-54171-1 £3.20 (including p & p)

ONE FAMILY'S WAR
A History of one family's experiences in World War II
Kisumu Books

Review by Faith Back, in 'Family Tree' magazine, March 2010 Issue –
'Sheila Wright decided to create a book recording her family's memories of the Second World War after her aunt loaned her a precious box of letters, diaries and other documents. The letters were written by the author's uncle, Brian Childs, a bomber pilot who was shot in 1941 after parachuting from his plane over France.

More treasured documents came to light supporting the stories and memories of other family members. These primary sources form the core of this marvellous tribute to one family's war service.

An excellent example of its kind, this beautifully produced book comprises more than 250 pages with black and white photographs and illustrations.'

The book contains extracts from the official battlefield Log Book of a Royal Artillery Regiment serving in North Africa, Italy and the Middle East between 1940-5, in which Jeffrey Childs (uncle of the author) served. Other personal accounts were contributed by relatives who grew up in South America.

Reading the stories inspired some younger members of the family to visit the war graves of their relatives for the first time. The book is an attempt to honour just a handful of the millions who served their country with such courage and selflessness in times of war.

Pat Kingsley, the Aunt whose loan of memorabilia was the motivation for this book said 'Your book is an absolute triumph and we are very proud to be such a part of it. You tell us lots of details that are absolutely new to me.... especially all the campaigns Jeff was involved in.'

Extract from a letter from David Childs who supplied despatches and a wartime diary relating the experiences of his father Major John Childs, in North Africa and Italy between 1941-45 –

'The book is great! The large format works really well. I feel as though I'm seeing the documents from my father for the first time and I've very much enjoyed the introduction to what has up to now been the 'lost' side of the family. The chapter on Brian really develops a sense of his life, and the sudden ending is something hard to imagine, growing up post-war.'

'My sister gave me a copy of 'One Family's War'. I LOVED IT. It was so fascinating I couldn't put it down!'

Beryl Roundhill, Vancouver, Canada

ISBN 978-0-9555417-3-5 £12.99 (plus p & p)

ESTANCIA LAS CORTADERAS
Saga of a Family and a Farm
Kisumu Books

This unusual book came about as a result of 'One Family's War'. Members of the author's extended family made contact after reading about their relatives' war service. A branch of family who had emigrated from the UK to South America, c.1908, shared their experiences and sent e-mails, diaries, letters and reminiscences from which the author compiled this saga of adventurous folk who braved stormy seas to start a new life in unknown territory.

The second chapter of the book tells of life in the English home counties in the 1880s and 1890s, where six Austin children grew up in the Mill House at a rural paper mill, with a charming but improvident father who struggled to maintain his family. Phyllis Austin tells how she travelled to France to become governess at a chateau, and later ventured into the slums of the East End as a midwife.

The back cover blurb reads – 'In 1908 Bert Austin, a young engineer, left his Hertfordshire home and sailed to Buenos Aires to work on the water and sewerage systems of that city. A few years later his sister Phyllis joined him. These two met another brother and sister, Harold and Aminta Bridger.

What happened next? Two marriages, a World War, ten children, an isolated estancia, drought, recession, another War, adventure holidays, forty grandchildren….

A fascinating story of intrepid, resourceful people, spanning over a century.'

A niece of Phyllis and Bert said 'I'm absolutely thrilled by this book. What a treasure, and so full of information and atmosphere…'

Pat Kingsley, Sussex, UK

A young Scots-Irish couple struggling to establish a farm, said 'We really enjoyed reading the book and soaked up the amazing tales from all the different family members. At times I was very moved by Phyllis and Harold's story and could strongly identify with the harsh journey of farming amid devastating drought or storms, battling against disease, locusts and financial difficulties….'

Isla and John Flanagan, France

Readers who had lived or stayed at the estancia praised the book -

'I read it straight through, there and then!…I loved it and am going to get one or two more for the family. They are a must. Thank you and congratulations for putting it all together…'

June Martin, Uruguay

'The book is beautifully put together, and beautifully edited….I am grateful for the light it shines on many of the family myths. Now we have some concrete evidence of the family dramas and of what lay behind them… '

Will Castleton, British Colombia

'A fantastic piece of work' - Mary Tara Marshall, Edinburgh, Scotland

'A story that had to be told' - Chris Nash, Oxfordshire, UK

'This is the story of pioneering days, the struggle of a family to establish itself and the tenacity needed to surmount adversity. One of the strongest characteristics of the Bridgers was the warmth of welcome that visitors were given, whether family or friends…..'

Jeremy Howat, Yorkshire, UK

'What I find fascinating is the family stories, their bravery, how they always travelled to faraway places, Argentina, India, Uruguay, UK, and got involved with the war too. The use of English governesses to such a large degree, education being paramount and costing them a fair bit… much of it pulls at the heart strings….'

Ted Palmer, UK

ISBN 978-0-9555417-6-6 £14.50 (plus p & p)

MURDER IN MEADOWFORD MAGNA
Kisumu Books
A short comedy murder play

Extract from Review –
'A body is found in the basement of the vicarage under a pile of coal.... The setting (the sleepy gardens of a Suffolk village), the time (1920s) and the many very British characters (squire, vicar, ex- colonials etc) is reminiscent of the stories of Agatha Christie.... Murder in Meadowford is good fun and highly entertaining.... the play reminds audiences of a time long ago when life seemed less complicated....a time that seems (at least in literature) a time of innocence...'

ISBN 978-0-9555417-4-2 £3.50 (including p & p)

MISCHIEF IN MEADOWFORD
Kisumu Books
A comedy play set in the same fictional Suffolk village c.1927

Extract from Review –
' The play starts with the deaths of two elderly eccentric sisters, who by mistake consume Fly Agaric mushrooms...... The mischief in this play takes place inside and outside an old mansion, home of the elderly Hepzibah Hamilton-Tracy when family and friends gather to celebrate her birthday.... In spite of the deaths, the play is good fun, largely because of the antics of those 'under the influence' at the cocktail party. Seeing them carrying on is bound to have the audience in stitches...'

These comedy playlets have been used in playreading sessions in Suffolk villages as an enjoyable way of raising funds for local projects. They are ideal for 'Who done it?' evenings in which, during a break between acts, refreshments are served while the audience write down their ideas about who did what, where, when, how and why. Prizes may be awarded at the end of the evening for the best, most comical, or most inventive answers.

ISBN 978-0-9555417-5-9 £3.50 (including p & p)

COMING SOON –

THE MEADOWFORD MYSTERIES – BOOK TWO
Mayhem at Wood Hall & Mallarky at St. Mildred's

HAUNTING TALES
paranormal experiences from Suffolk, England

HOW TO ORDER

To order any of Sheila's books, see website www.kisumubooks.co.uk
Please e-mail the author for p & p costs, and details of generous discounts for
any purchase of more than one book. The prices given above are a guide only.

Email: sheronkis@hotmail.co.uk